The Birthday Romance Collection

By Rachel Rinetti

This is a work of fiction. Characters, events and places are are a figment of the author's imagination, or are used fictitiously.

ISBN 978-0-6450793-1-9

For Mum.

BIRTHDAY GIRL

Book one

SOME BIRTHDAY WISHES DO COME TRUE

CHAPTER ONE

The silver Honda screeched to a halt on the gravel driveway, sending rocks flying into the air.

'Lizzie, for crying out loud!' Angie grabbed the seatbelt to stop herself from launching straight through the windscreen.

'Sorry. I might still be a little drunk from last night,' Lizzie quipped, almost proud of herself.

Angie glared at her best friend. They'd been out on the town the night before. It was an invitation Angie had begrudgingly accepted at five thirty on Friday afternoon. Like always, Lizzie had a good time dancing and binge drinking before passing out on Angie's couch in her work clothes. Angie had offered to drive today, but Lizzie insisted her birthday trip be kept a secret until they arrived at the mystery location.

'Here we are,' Lizzie announced.

They both sat in the humming Honda and Angie leaned towards the windscreen to take a look around. They were in the country alright, but for what? Lizzie still hadn't let the secret slip.

To the left of the driveway stood an old homestead. The orange brick reminded Angie of the terracotta pots her mum used for outdoor plants. The freshly mown grass was complimented by a garden of natives and a hedge of lavender running around the perimeter of the fence. A small birdbath sat in the corner of the backyard, soaking up the shade of the old, giant gum trees. A kookaburra perched on the edge, dipping its beak into the water for a drink.

There was a sign on the gate, swaying to the rhythm of the wind.

'Brumby-spotting?' Angie asked.

'You betcha. What's better than riding a horse? Riding a tame horse while you spot *wild* horses in their natural habitat. Pretty cool, huh?'

The leaves of a large gum tree hung over a faded green shed to the right of the gravel driveway.

Three kookaburras sat on a branch humming their koo-kaas. The kookaburra in the bird bath swooped to the ground before flying majestically to the branch where the others were sitting.

'Ooo la la. Looks like we might have a cowboy on our hands today,' Lizzie cooed and pointed to a lone man in dark blue jeans, a black and red flannelette shirt, and an Akubra hat to finish off the look.

Angie swallowed.

A cowboy?

Could he hear her thoughts? He turned around and headed towards them. His boots clicked against the gravel and he held a rope in either hand with a tight grip, forcing the veins in his forearms to pop. Wispy brunette hair sat underneath the Akubra, and his tan resembled butterscotch.

'He's coming this way. Let's roll.' Lizzie opened the driver door.

She swung both legs outside and stood to attention. There was nothing left to protest. They were here, and this was happening, so Angie followed her friend's lead.

'It *is* a real cowboy,' Lizzie attempted to whisper over the car.

'Shhh,' Angie replied, hoping he hadn't heard Lizzie's comment.

'Nice to make your acquaintance, ladies. I'm Liam and I'll be your tour guide today,' the cowboy said as he offered his hand.

Lizzie shot Angie a glance before stepping forward to introduce herself.

'I'm Lizzie and this is my friend, Angie. We're looking forward to the sights. And of course, the horses.'

The horses!

The reality was now settling in. Angie didn't think anyone, especially Lizzie, would actually go through with making her birthday wish a reality. Now Angie had bigger problems to worry about. How was she going to get on the horse? Would it turn wild and run away, or buck her off and leave her lying in a hospital bed?

Thoughts of what could go wrong forced her to hold her breath. As a lawyer, Angie didn't take risks. She did her research to pursue the best strategy for her clients. This adventure Lizzie had planned was riddled with risks, especially for someone who'd never even patted a horse, let alone sat in a saddle before.

'You must be Angie.' A large hand reached out as the cowboy stood in front of her. A smile emerged on his face, showing off deep dimples. Had he just stepped off the scene of a country western film? He oozed charm, like the leading man in a newly-released blockbuster film.

The stubble on his face gave him a rugged, bad-boy aura, as did the strands of chest hair puffing from under his flannelette shirt.

The scent of lavender, hay and a hint of aftershave assaulted Angie's nostrils. There was no way she would lose her composure in front of this cowboy.

Pull yourself together, woman.

'Yep, that's me.' Angie stepped forward to shake his hand.

Their hands seemed to fit perfectly together. Angie could've stayed there forever, holding his hand and staring into his grey, cloudy eyes. Something about him was warm and familiar, like she could have an actual conversation with him. Not like the other dates she'd been on recently.

'Have you ridden a horse before?' Liam asked.

'Heaps of times,' Lizzie replied.

'I have *not*,' Angie added, trying to sound professional but coming off slightly pompous.

'That's no problem at all. We've got the perfect horse for you.'

'Great, because I'm a little scared...actually I'm scared senseless scared right now.'

'It's her birthday today too,' Lizzie added with a wink.

Angie glared at her best friend again.

'Well, Happy Birthday,' Liam said with a huge grin. 'The bureau has forecast late showers today, but we'll be fine until early afternoon.'

Angie glanced up and noticed clouds forming in the distance. They didn't seem to be cause for concern, but Mother Nature was unpredictable.

'Liam!'

The deep voice took Angie by surprise. As she looked over Liam's shoulder, an older man wandered down the footpath from the house with a slight limp in his walk.

'Time to get the horses or we'll be running behind schedule,' the man said in a low, gruff voice as he shooed a fly from his face.

'Sure thing, Dad.' Liam turned back to Angie and smiled. 'Alright, ladies, let's get this show on the road.'

* * *

Lizzie must've been listening when Angie had said she wanted to ride a horse for her birthday. Of course Angie wasn't serious. She really just wanted something to complain about since every other birthday had been a total let down. A nice birthday dinner and a chick flick would've sufficed. Now, because of her big mouth, she was standing in someone's outback driveway getting ready to ride an animal that could very well kill her.

'He's pretty cute.'

'What?'

'The cowboy. Hot. Earth to Angie,' Lizzie teased as she waved her hands in front of Angie's face.

It was all a bit of a shock. Coming to the Snowy Mountains to ride a horse still hadn't settled in, and her mind was distracted by the unfamiliar place.

'Yes, he's cute,' Angie replied without a second thought.

'I knew it. Your first visit to the country and you already want to ride a cowboy.'

'Lizzie!' Angie slapped her friend across the arm. She wasn't a prude, but she hated broadcasting anything to do with her deep dark desires to the world.

'I know you too well, horny birthday girl. I'm sure if you ask nicely he might give you something else to ride,' Lizzie replied with a wink.

Angie rolled her eyes and stepped away from her friend. 'I can't take you anywhere. Not everything has to be sexual, Elizabeth. For once can you get your damned head out of the gutter and try to enjoy something without turning it into a talk of dicks?'

Lizzie silenced and her smile flattened. Someone was watching them. Angie pinched her eyes shut, hoping Liam hadn't heard what she'd said. For all she knew, his dick was perfectly sizeable.

When she opened her eyes, it was worse. It was his old man.

'Well, don't stop talking about dicks on my account,' he sniggered as he fixed the Akubra hat on his head and limped towards the green shed.

Angie pursed her lips together. She was only one step away from seriously considering sewing them shut. Could she be anymore inappropriate? Christ, the old man probably thought he was taking a bunch of sex-deprived singletons for a horse ride into the bush.

'Liam might be just what you need. I mean, it has been two years,' Lizzie said with a nudge of her elbow.

Angie didn't need the reminder. It was on this day two years ago the man she thought she was destined to spend the rest of her life with broke up with her instead. On her birthday. For another woman. Who was also three months pregnant.

'Thanks for that lovely trip down memory lane. Shall we reflect on all the other failures in my life?'

Lizzie waved her hand in the air. 'Craig was never good enough for you anyway. You're better off without him.'

It was too late. Angie couldn't shake the idea that she was a fraud. That she was trying too hard. That she was, in fact, a failure. When she looked down at her outfit, she didn't like what she saw. Light blue, fitted jeans followed the curves of her body and hugged right down to her ankles.

The white canvas runners were totally out of place on the dusty farm, and she didn't even want to think about the vomit green polo shirt she'd thrown on this morning. What was she supposed to wear horse riding anyway?

Lizzie hadn't dressed any better. At least Angie had been somewhat practically. Lizzie had gone full glam with ripped designer jeans and a pink satin shirt that gave her skin barely any sun protection.

Angie didn't know anything about horses and her friend, who was equally oblivious, had dragged her out here for a brumby-spotting tour with zero notice. There was no time to research or prepare.

Who was she kidding? She'd probably suffer sunburn and have a chaffing rash between her thighs from sitting in the saddle all day. Telling Lizzie about her birthday wish was a mistake. Now she was going to have to go through with it, and likely make a complete idiot of herself.

'Maybe this wasn't such a good idea,' she said as Lizzie locked the car. 'I think we should go home and book a massage. Maybe go to dinner afterwards.'

Lizzie stopped walking and pressed her palms against the waistband of her designer jeans. 'What do you mean we should go home? This is what you wanted for your birthday. *You* wanted to ride a horse and that's what I'm giving you. You can't back out now.'

'Yes, but—'

'Okay, ladies. Your horses are ready.' Liam walked towards them along the gravel driveway with a rope in each hand. Only this time, there were horses attached to those ropes.

The backdrop was Hollywood-worthy. The curves of the green mountains made an impeccable green screen, and a hunky man was making his way towards her with two beautiful horses by his side.

A black horse walked on one side, and a chestnut on the other. The chestnut was taller, more athletic, and the black one reminded her of the horse in Black Beauty.

'They're beautiful,' she whispered as they made their way towards her, their hooves clip clopping against the gravel.

Liam stopped a metre away. 'Don't be shy. Come say hello. The black one is Beauty. And the chestnut is Magic.'

'Beauty. What a perfect name,' Angie replied.

Lizzie was less than impressed at the sight before them. 'Ugh, I didn't realise they'd smell so bad.'

'What did you expect? They're horses,' Angie said.

'I know they're horses. They still stink.' Lizzie crossed her arms across her chest. 'I think I'll stand back for now.'

'Suit yourself.' Angie took a hesitant step forward, holding her hands out to the horses. Both Beauty and Magic seemed eager to greet her. They reached their necks out to sniff her hand and Beauty nibbled and licked her skin. The horses were majestic, gentle. But their presence made her heart beat at a furious pace. Mum had always said horses were dangerous. It was why she never got the chance to ride one as a child.

'It's alright,' Liam encouraged. 'They're harmless.'

'I really...I'm not good with horses. I've never been this close.'

Liam dropped the ropes onto the gravel driveway. He reached his hands under the necks of both horses and began scratching their cheeks. Both horses tossed their heads in the air with delight as Liam scratched down their necks.

'You give these guys a pat and they'll be your best friend for life.

Like a dog really, only bigger.'

'And smellier,' Lizzie added.

Angie stepped closer to the horses and ran her hands down their faces. The silky hair was smooth under her palms, and their coats glimmered under the warmth of the April sun.

'See, nothing to worry about,' Liam said.

Angie caught Liam's eyes, crinkling in the corners. But not at her. These horses clearly held a special place in his heart. It was nice, standing in this stranger's driveway in the middle of the country, watching the way he looked at his horses.

A quick pulse flickered between her legs. Angie held her breath and looked away.

Was that what I think it was? Is this guy turning me on?

'Ugh, gross,' Lizzie cried as the chestnut opened its bowels on the driveway.

Angie looked over her shoulder and glared at Lizzie. Angie looked back at Liam and smiled. 'They're perfect.'

'I think Beauty likes you,' Liam replied. 'Would you like to take over from here? I need to get four more horses from the paddock for the tour.'

'Ah...I don't know if I'm ready. What if she runs away?'

Liam picked up the rope and held it in front of him. 'She won't run away. And even if she does there are fences around the property. She can't go far.'

Angie stared into his eyes for a brief moment. They sloped slightly at the corners, making his face appear soft and kind.

When Angie reached out her hand to take the rope from him, their fingers touched. He didn't immediately pull away, and neither did she.

'I guess I'll take my horse too,' Lizzie said, interrupting the moment.

Angie took the rope from Liam's hand while Lizzie grabbed Magic's rope. Liam turned towards the paddock and Angie stared at the jeans pulled tight around his behind. He clearly worked outdoors with an ass like that.

She was ashamed to admit she hadn't let a man touch her in the last two years. But she was still grieving the betrayal of her ex boyfriend, who was now married with baby number two on the way.

'Dad, you need to rest. You shouldn't be out here,' Angie heard

Liam say in the distance.

'Don't be ludicrous. I'll rest when I'm dead. Just get Clancy for me, would you?' the old man argued as he hobbled along the driveway.

'You be careful with your attitude, old man, or I'll start calling you Watson again...'

'Ahh, the sounds of bickering families,' Lizzie announced. 'Nothing better, I say.'

The timber front door of the house slammed shut and a loved-up couple walked out holding hands. Clearly thinking they couldn't be seen, the man grabbed the woman, pecking her on the neck and pulling her hips into his.

'Woah, just what I need to see on a Saturday morning with a hangover,' Lizzie said.

'Who are they?' Angie asked.

'They must've done the overnight trip where you stay in the homestead and ride through the bush the next day.'

'I feel sorry for whoever was sleeping in the room next to them last night,' Angie muttered.

The man now had his hand up the woman's shirt and they were dry humping on the brick wall next to the front door.

'We can see you!' Lizzie shouted, while Beauty and Magic grazed at the side of the driveway.

The couple looked around and when they spotted Lizzie and Angie, they pulled themselves together and walked down the footpath like two perfectly respectable people.

'Good morning,' the man said in an Italian accent.

'We just got married and we're on our honeymoon. This is my *amore*.'

'Nice to meet you,' Angie replied, wishing she could say *she* was married.

When the couple had their backs turned, Lizzie said, 'Ugh, don't you just hate seeing loved-up couples in public? Makes me sick to my stomach.'

It *did* make Angie sick to her stomach, but only because she wanted that for herself.

A sound of thunder blew up from behind the shed. The two horses jumped and craned their necks around to check out the commotion.

A rusty, off-white horse truck emerged from behind the shed, and the diesel engine pumped black smoke into the air as it stopped in the middle of the driveway.

Lizzie coughed and waved a hand in front of her face. 'Jesus, that thing needs a mechanic.'

'Don't be ridiculous,' the old man replied as he jumped out of the cab. 'This old girl's been going strong for twenty years. There's no stopping her now,' he said as he patted the hood of the truck.

'Come on, quit holding us up,' the old man called out to Liam who was walking two horses through a gate. 'We're behind schedule.'

'Alright, keep your pants on, Watson,' Liam called back.

The old man headed over to the gate to put a halter on two more horses, who were standing in a holding paddock next to the shed, now making six horses ready for the trip.

'All ready, birthday girl?' Liam asked as he approached. His hand brushed Angie's as he grabbed Beauty's rope.

A spark of electricity shot up her arm, bringing her entire body to life.

Angie smiled and tucked a loose strand of blonde hair behind her ear. 'As ready as I'll ever be.'

CHAPTER TWO

Angie sat snug between Liam and Lizzie in the truck while Liam's old man, Watson, and the two Italian lovebirds followed in a ute behind them.

It had been a long time since Angie had been this close to a man, and it was taking its toll. Sweaty palms made it hard to grip the leather seats, so she resorted to holding onto Lizzie instead when the truck careened around tight corners.

'Sorry for the mess in the cab. My brother's a bit of a slob at the best of times. And old Watson doesn't help the situation either.'

The inside of the cab resembled landfill at the local tip. The floor was covered in bits of paper, tissues, empty bottles of coke, and farming magazines were strewn all over the dashboard.

'Brother, huh,' Lizzie replied. 'That's what they all say.'

'I wish I was lying. I only came down this morning from Canberra because my brother's got a severe case of gastro and couldn't take the tour.'

'It's not that messy,' Angie lied, not wanting to linger on the topic of gastro too long.

She glanced in Liam's direction and admired his strong shoulders steering the truck underneath the flannelette shirt.

Liam crunched the truck into the next gear and steered it onto a dirt road. Angie spotted the veins in his arms pop as he maneuvered the steering wheel.

She was able to keep her desire under wraps on the open bitumen road, but when they hit the dirt road, she faced a different dilemma. There were potholes and tight turns, and each time Liam steered the truck to avoid them, she bumped into him, their arms and legs touching each other over and over again. Each time their bodies met, it was like an unbearable mosquito bite she couldn't resist scratching.

If only Lizzie wasn't here.

Then Angie might've garnered the courage to reach out and touch Liam the way she wanted to.

'So, Liam. What do you do for work?' Lizzie asked, finally breaking the silence.

'Well, this is a family business and I help where I can. But I actually live and work in Canberra.'

'You don't say,' Lizzie replied with a smirk as she glanced at Angie. 'We're from Canberra.'

'A great place to live.'

'And coming back to help on the farm? Your girlfriend must be so proud of you.'

'Yeah, my imaginary girlfriend?' Liam laughed as he steered the truck around another sharp corner.

Lizzie chuckled, overacting the whole thing. 'Well, this is perfect. Because you know who else is single? Angie.'

* * *

'You're the worst friend, you hear me? Why did you have to embarrass me like that?' Angie whispered as they slid across the cab and jumped out of the truck.

The grass was soft beneath Angie's shoes as she landed on the grass. When she looked up, the view of the mountains was more serene, more dramatic than she could've ever imagined. The mountains curved into one another in the distance, and the gum trees stood several metres above them. It would be easy to get lost in the view.

'Why am I the worst friend? Because I said you were single? It's not a lie, and besides who cares? What do you care what he thinks of you, unless...'

Lizzie, don't you dare say it.

'Unless you think he's hot and you want to bang him.'

Angie rolled her eyes and stormed past Lizzie to the tailgate of the truck. Of course Angie thought Liam was hot. Plus, he'd been nothing but a gentleman since they'd arrived. That was enough to get her interested. And it was definitely more than she could say of any of the men she'd gone on dates with in the last two years. At least this one could hold a conversation without making everything sexual.

'Maybe another birthday wish will come true, if you're lucky,' Lizzie teased.

'Is it your birthday today?'

Angie looked across at the Italian woman standing with her husband at the side of the truck. The woman's long brunette hair was slicked back in a low ponytail over her shoulder, and the skin-tight jeans and black skivvy exaggerated her slim frame.

'Ah, yeah,' Angie replied. 'It's my birthday. Twenty-eight today.'

'Only two years from thirty,' Lizzie added.

'Bella, that's so lovely. Buon Compleanno.'

'Huh?' Lizzie questioned.

'It's happy birthday in Italian, dummy,' Angie whispered.

The Italian woman didn't seem to take any notice of the comment. 'We're on our honeymoon,' she said as she tugged at the collar of her husband's shirt and growled like a hungry tiger. 'We were married two weeks ago in Venice with our families. The best day of our lives. And now we're here to explore this beautiful country. We've always wanted to come.' The woman kissed her husband on the lips, and he wrapped his arms around her tiny waist.

'Congratulations,' Lizzie replied in a sarcastic tone.

Angie forced a smile, and resisted the urge to find the nearest tree to throw up. 'Yes, congratulations,' she reiterated in her most formal voice, as the couple continued to rub their hands all over each other.

If only I could be so lucky.

'Alright, first cab off the rank is Beauty,' Liam announced as he walked down the tailgate with the black horse in tow. Even though she was a little sweaty, she seemed in good spirits from the thirty-minute trip. And Liam looked like a cowboy straight out of a romance novel leading her off the truck. That hat and killer smile had Angie feeling a little light-headed.

Angie tugged at her vomit green polo shirt to try and get some air into her lungs.

'Here you go.' Liam held out the rope.

Angie stepped forward to take it.

'Tie her up at the front of the truck and I'll help you get saddled.' He placed his hand in the curve of her back and pointed to the metal hook closest to the driver door. 'Right there.'

For the first time in two years, Angie didn't flinch at the male contact.

When Liam's hand left her body, she pushed aside the urge to grab it and place it back where it was a moment ago. Instead, she led Beauty to the front of the truck as she was told.

She wrapped the rope through the loop at the side of the truck and patted the mare's neck. She still couldn't believe how close she was to a horse. Maybe this birthday wouldn't be so bad after all.

* * *

'All you need to do is lift your left leg and I'll give you a boost into the saddle.'

'Are you sure I won't weigh—'

'Of course you won't weigh too much. I've done this for burly men a hundred times before. You've got nothing to worry about.' Liam brushed past her to tighten the girth of the saddle.

Angie's eyes closed and she breathed in the smell of fresh hay and cologne he left lingering behind.

'Are you ready?'

Angie opened her eyes and nodded.

'You need to put your hands up here and hold on tight.' He grabbed both her hands and placed them on the pommel of the saddle.

There's that electricity again.

He looked down into her eyes and smiled. 'On the count of three, you're going to bounce off your right leg and I'm going to lift. Okay?'

'Okay.'

With her hands held tight around the pommel of the saddle, she tentatively lifted her left leg. Liam bent at the knees, wrapped his hands under her leg, and on the count of three, lifted her into the saddle. She felt light as a feather as she flew into the air and onto the horse's back.

'Told you it would be fine.' For some reason, his hand remained on her thigh. Angie's breath caught in her throat.

'Just try to relax. The more relaxed you are, the more relaxed Beauty will be. If you tense up, she might think something's wrong.'

'You ready to go?' The old man called out from the back of the truck.

'Yep,' Liam replied as he took his hand off Angie's leg and stepped over to his own horse. 'Gather up the reins so you have some control.'

'How does it work?' Angie held up the reins by the buckle, not quite sure how to hold them. 'Are you going to lead me?'

'If you'd feel more comfortable.'

Angie's poker face had clearly let her down. 'I'd feel *much* more comfortable.'

Liam smiled. 'Sure thing. Just let me get sorted.'

Angie watched as he tightened the girth. There were those forearm veins again, popping as he secured the saddle. He wiped the back of his hand over his forehead before pulling the Akubra back onto his head.

Yikes.

'Alright, everyone, follow me.' The old man rode up front, taking the lead. Liam hung back with Angie and Lizzie.

'Guess I'll go ahead then,' Lizzie complained. She pushed her horse to walk and held up the reins like a child on the back of a camel.

Angie didn't know what to do. Where did the reins go? Was she chaffing already? In the courtroom against ruthless lawyers she was unshakeable. But in the saddle, she had no control of the situation.

'I don't know if I can do this.' The breaths became shallow in her chest.

'Do what?' Liam asked.

'This.' Never in her life had she felt like such a fraud. 'This is utterly mortifying,' she whispered, still holding the reins by the buckle.

'Why is it mortifying?' Liam questioned as he clipped a leading rein onto Beauty's bridle.

'Because I feel like a toddler at a school fete on a grumpy pony. I'm not ready for this.'

Liam hung back with Angie while the other riders walked out onto the bush track.

'It can be scary, sure. But you're not a toddler and Beauty's definitely not a grumpy pony. No harm in trying something scary every once in a while. Test your limits. And if you need me to, I can lead you the whole way.'

'You'd do that?'

'Of course. This is your special day,' he said with a smile.

Maybe chivalry isn't dead after all.

The panic dissipated and her heartbeat began to beat at a regular pace. 'Okay, I guess I can give it a try.'

* * *

Almost an hour had passed. Liam and Angie followed the riders and their horses as they followed the winding track through the bush. Liam's horse, Max, and Beauty walked close together, forcing Angie and Liam's legs to rub against each other. She needed something to take her mind off the physical contact.

'Is that a mustang?' the Italian woman called out.

Everyone looked to their left, just in time to spot a herd of brumbies galloping through a cluster of trees and down towards a riverbank. There were so many colours, and some were only foals.

'They're beautiful,' Angie whispered.

'That sky doesn't look promising,' The old man called out to the group.

When Angie looked up, the overcast clouds were beginning to descend over the bush. 'Rain wasn't forecast for today. Only later tonight,' Liam replied.

'Oh!' called out the Italian woman at the front of the group. 'I felt a raindrop.'

The old man stopped his horse in the middle of the track and the others almost walked into the back of him. He put his finger in his mouth and held it up to the sky. When he looked to the back of the group, the lines in his forehead had deepened.

'The wind's picking up. We need to head back,' he said.

'So soon?' the Italian woman asked. 'But we just got here.'

'Tomorrow,' the old man replied in a gruff voice. 'It's too dangerous for beginners to ride in a storm. We'll come out again when the sky clears. Right now, we need to get to shelter.' The old man reigned his horse around and looped back past Angie and Liam.

'Dad, just keep it slow, okay? I've got Beauty on a lead and—'

'There's no time, son. Just get Beauty and Max back to the truck so we can try to miss this storm and get everyone back to the homestead.'

The others followed at a trot, including Lizzie who was bouncing up and down in the saddle, while Liam tried to turn Max and Beauty around. Beauty took a step forward when a crash of thunder belted down to earth and bellowed through the valley.

The horse froze underneath Angie. 'Oh no.'

Beauty lifted her head and looked at the sky. Her ears flickered back and forth. The rain started to spit and thunder began to rumble through the Snowy Mountains.

Angie pressed her heels into the mare's stomach. Nothing. 'She won't move,' Angie said as her heart started to pump at an accelerated pace in her chest.

'Come on, Beauty,' Liam said as he pulled on the leading rein. The horse wouldn't budge.

The rain started to pelt to earth in large droplets.

'This isn't good,' Angie declared. 'This isn't good at all!'

CHAPTER THREE

Oh. My. God.

The words raced through Angie's mind on repeat. The rain was now bucketing down, drenching her clothes, and she couldn't make Beauty move.

The shallow breaths and racing thoughts Liam had told her to push aside were back in full force. So much adrenaline pumped through her veins. So many goosebumps covered her skin at the touch of the cold rain. She tried to push the horse forward without success. Beauty was frozen, stunned by the storm.

'Why isn't she moving?' Angie cried.

'I don't know. She's never done this before,' Liam replied as he tugged gently on the lead. It was no use. It was as if Beauty was stuck in quicksand and sinking fast. The rain was almost blinding now and stung as it hit Angie's face. Liam jumped off his horse and threw the stirrups over the saddle.

'What're you doing?'

'She's not leading off the other horse. I have to lead her on foot.'

'What? We've been out here for over an hour. There's no way you can run that far on foot.'

'I'll damn well try.' He pulled the reins over his horse's head and grabbed a tighter hold of Beauty's reins.

When Angie put her hands on the mare's neck, the horse was shaking from the chill of the rain.

'What're we going to do? She isn't moving.'

Liam walked up to Beauty's face, stroked his hands down her cheeks and whispered something in her ear. He continued to stroke, slow strokes. Angie couldn't hear what he was saying amongst the falling rain, and it was wasting precious time.

'We need to get out of here before we get struck by lightning!' Angie cried.

Liam turned on his feet and tugged at the leading rein. Beauty stepped off, following his direction.

Is he a horse whisperer?

There was no time to dwell on the question. Hail was pelting down and hitting them like rogue balls at a golfing tournament. It took all of Angie's strength not to scream. So much for a great birthday. This had to be the worst one yet.

She held on to the saddle for dear life as Liam zig-zagged in between trees, up and down embankments and amongst the shrubs, and she bounced up and down in the saddle. Beauty and Max trotted after Liam, who was near sprinting now while weaving through the bush. Angie looked up from under her helmet and spotted a small brick hut.

Why not back to the truck?

A large rod of lighting struck the earth nearby and a branch cracked and crashed to the ground.

When they reached the hut, Liam gave Angie an order. 'Take your feet out of the stirrups.'

She did as she was told.

'Swing your leg over and jump off.'

Again, Angie did as Liam said. She dropped into a puddle of water and it soaked her canvas shoes.

Liam pulled the reins over Beauty's head and led both horses under a corrugated iron shelter that sloped off the small brick hut. It wasn't much, but at least it provided them with some respite from the storm.

Liam opened the door of the hut and Angie rushed inside. It wasn't as shabby as she was expecting, but it certainly wasn't a five-star hotel. A single bed sat in the corner alongside a stove and a miniature fireplace.

Liam rushed inside and kicked the door closed behind him. He was holding a saddle in each arm. His hair dripped at the ends leaving a trail of water behind him. The sight of him drenched, his hair wild and his clothes soaked, left Angie's throat dry.

'That's one crazy storm out there,' he managed to say through quick, shallow breaths.

'Are the horses okay?'

'They're tied up where it's dry under the corrugated iron. They'll be fine.'

A weight released at the confession, but now there was another challenge. She couldn't take her eyes off the man standing in front of her. His hair was saturated from the rain and his clothes clung to his muscled body.

Liam dropped the saddles next to the door and shook his head. The water spattered onto the walls.

'What is this place?' Angie asked, looking around.

'It's a hut my brother, Dad and I built for times like these when we got stuck in a storm.'

It seemed hardly big enough for three people.

'When can we get back to the farm?'

'We won't be going anywhere for a while. Did you see that branch fall down after being struck by lightning? That could've been you or me and I don't think either of us want that.'

That'd be the cherry on top for the birthday from hell.

Liam pulled a mobile from his pocket and pressed it to his ear. 'Crap. Voicemail. Hey, Dad. Angie and I are at the hut and we're safe. Just waiting for the storm to pass over. Once it's passed we'll ride back to the truck.' He sighed as he hung up and slid the phone into the pocket of his jeans. 'I'm sorry the trip didn't turn out how you expected. But heck, at least you'll have a story to tell the grandkids one day.'

Maybe it was her soaked, shivering body, the genuine kindness in Liam's eyes, or the caring tone in his voice. Whatever it was, something tipped her over the edge. Before she could stop herself, the tears escaped, streaming down her face.

'I'm sorry, is it something I said?'

Angie waved her hand in the air as she tried to hold back tears. 'No, nothing you said. I just can't believe this birthday turned out exactly the same as all my other birthdays. Complete shit.'

'It's not anyone's fault this storm came over without warning.'

'I know that. But why today? There are three hundred and sixty-four other days for this to happen. Why my birthday?'

Liam stood still for a moment and glanced around the hut. A moment later, he stepped forward and put his arms around Angie's shoulders. They were both drenched, and Angie was shaking.

Yet despite the unfortunate circumstances, it was comforting being held in a man's arms, against a strong, broad chest. She lifted her arms and wrapped them around his waist. The smell of wet hay and cologne overtook her senses. It was dangerous. This man was luring her in.

'Life is like that sometimes. That's all there is to it.' Instead of letting her go, or telling her to get over herself, which she'd heard so many times before, he embraced her.

'How old are you?'

'Twenty-five.'

Three years her junior. Yet somehow so full of wisdom.

You're doing it again. Letting crazy thoughts about this sexy man control your mind.

It was worse now they were in a confined space and his hands were on her body.

'I think we should take off some of these clothes,' he suggested as his arms dropped away.

'Excuse me?' Angie froze at his remark. He wasn't suggesting...

'Even though it's nice seeing those wet clothes cling to your body, I think you'd be more comfortable in something dry.'

Oh.

Liam rummaged through a plastic tub on the floor.

'Do you know what happened to the others? I hope they're okay.'

Liam pulled out a few items of clothing. 'They likely found their way back to the truck. They'll be safe there.'

Angie wrapped her arms around her wet body. A distinct chill set in her bones. 'How long will it take to pass?'

Liam paused and listened to the rain on the roof. 'At least another hour, maybe more. The worst of the storm might be over, but it's still wet. That can be a real danger for the horses. One slip and someone will get hurt.' He handed Angie an oversized shirt and mustard-coloured tracksuit pants.

Liam and Angie stood face-to-face, his grey eyes staring down into hers.

'Can I have some privacy while I change?'

'Of course, sure.' Liam spun around. Instead of waiting for Angie to take off her clothes, he began undressing himself.

First, he took off the flannelette shirt, then the white singlet underneath. He peeled it away from his skin and over his head. The muscles in his back flexed as he grabbed a fresh shirt from the tub. Pulling it over his head, it caught on his wet shoulders. Without turning around, he grabbed at the shirt behind his back to pull it down, showing off more skin than Angie could handle.

'Can I turn around yet?'

'Ah, just a minute.' She changed hastily and then gave him the okay to turn around.

'You pull off that outfit better than anyone I know.'

'You've got to be joking. The oversized t-shirt doesn't really suit these mustard tracky daks.

'Hungry?'

'Maybe a little.'

'Let me serve you some lukewarm tinned spaghetti for lunch. It's a fan favourite around here. We'd normally serve a hot lunch at the truck, but given this weather, tinned spaghetti will have to do.' Liam grabbed two tins from the plastic container, a box of matches and a few pieces of kindling.

'Not going to light the fire the old-fashioned way by rubbing two sticks together?'

'Why would I do that when I have matches?' he replied with a smile.

Duh.

Angie sat next to the stove on the floor, cross-legged and watched the flames flicker and spit. It wasn't a powerful fire, but it was kind of romantic.

'What do you do back in Canberra?'

'I'm a lawyer.' Angie was proud of her career. It was a dream she'd had since she was a little girl, but sometimes she found men were put off by it. The job wasn't a nurturing role. Most days she had to be ruthless. She was a fighter, loved a good argument, but that didn't sit well with the guys she'd dated over the past two years. The ones who were threatened by her confidence and independence.

'That's awesome. I bet you're a great lawyer.'

The yearning for his touch grew stronger. She'd been able to push it aside earlier today around the group. But with the rain pelting down outside, the small fire, and their damp bodies covered in stranger's clothing, desire swirled in the deepest part of her.

Liam poured the tinned spaghetti into a bowl and passed it to her. The bowl hovered above her crossed legs. There was nothing to lose. Nothing.

Except for rejection.

The thought made her stop for a moment. Could she really sit with him, potentially for a few more hours, with the knowledge he didn't feel the same way?

Oh, stuff it.

With the way this birthday was going, it couldn't really get any worse.

She reached out and touched his arm, her fingers gliding down his wrist and over his hand.

He stared down at her hand, before looking up.

'Liam. We're stuck in this hut for God only knows how long. It could be hours for all we know.'

He looked down at her hand again. 'What're you trying to say?'

There was no point being sophisticated, or even ladylike at this point. Angie had an itch that needed to be scratched. And hopefully Liam was the man for the job.

'It's my birthday and I haven't been with anyone in over two years. This birthday has already turned to shit, but I'm hoping you might be able to turn it around.' She paused, eager for him to take the hint. When he didn't respond she elaborated.

'Sexually.'

Liam didn't hesitate. He put his bowl down and reached his hand to hers, pulling her to her feet. Standing, he was a whole head taller than her and she had to stand on her tippy toes so their lips could touch.

'That's very forward of you, Angie,' he breathed quietly.

'But from the looks of it you don't hate the idea,' she whispered back. She stroked her hand down his face.

The stubble of his chin prickled her fingertips. Then those same lips that breathed the words met hers. She melted into the kiss, almost losing her balance completely. But this strong cowboy kept her steady on her feet.

When her head tilted back, she moaned as he kissed slowly down her neck, licking and kissing the sensitive skin around her collarbone. Her whole body tingled at the touch of his lips.

This is what she'd been missing out on for two years? He grabbed the collar of her oversized t-shirt and pulled it down, exposing her cleavage. The kisses between her breasts forced goose bumps to rise over her skin. The yearning between her thighs surged.

Oh God.

'Liam,' she breathed into his ear. 'I want you now.'

Liam traced his fingers down her spine and over her butt, before pulling her up along his body. She leaned down to kiss him as her legs wrapped around his waist.

'Are you sure you want to do this? Two years is a long time to not —'

Angie pressed her finger on his lips. 'I was just waiting for the right guy.'

In one swift motion he lay her down onto the single bed. The springs creaked underneath them.

Angie giggled. 'How old is this bed?'

'Too old to sleep in, but not too old for this.' Without hesitation, Liam slowly slid the mustard-coloured tracksuit pants down her legs, forcing every inch of her skin to come alive.

Thank God I remembered to shave.

He kissed the inside of her thighs, making her squirm and giggle. The sensation of his lips on her skin was electrifying. But was she out of her depth? She'd never had a one-night stand and was about to have sex in an outback hut with a cowboy she'd just met. It was too much. Way too much. But the pleasure was taking control and she didn't want it to stop.

She sat up and kissed him. As she ran her hands down his body, she pulled off his shirt. Once off, it revealed the hard-working body she'd been dying to see since she'd first laid eyes on him.

He paused. 'Is this okay? I don't want you to do something you might regret.'

'Regret?' Angie stopped and stared into his grey eyes. 'Do *you* want to stop?'

'Hell no. But I wouldn't forgive myself if *you* regretted this afterwards.'

Angie pondered the thought a moment. Chivalry certainly wasn't dead with Liam. But maybe he was right. Maybe she wasn't ready for this.

'I have an idea.' Liam threw her pants off the bed and positioned himself between her legs.

'What're you doing?'

'Helping to relieve some of that stress.' He kissed the inside of her thighs again, and her head tilted back as she grabbed onto his hair. As he got closer, she tried to wriggle from his grip, but he wouldn't let go. When his mouth finally connected with her, her back arched and her head tilted back into the pillow.

Liam!

It was warm. So warm. As his tongue swirled, his hands followed the curves of her body, lingering on her hips, leaving no inch of skin untouched.

Two years. Two fucking years.

Craig had never touched her this way. He'd never given her his full attention the way Liam did.

It only took a few minutes for the strokes, the swirls, the circles of pleasure from Liam's tongue to take her over the edge. Within an instant, the warmth spread through her whole body, calming her mind completely. Her body melted into the bed.

Liam pulled himself up and lay his head on the pillow next to her.

'I hope you don't still think this is the worst birthday ever,' he said as he stroked a piece of hair behind her ear.

Angie turned her face towards him. It wasn't the first time she'd been on the receiving end, but it had definitely been longer than two years. And she didn't remember it ever being that intense. She could've laid with Liam for hours, letting the calm of the moment overtake them.

'I think—'

A ringing phone interrupted them. 'Ignore it,' Liam said.

'It could be important,' she replied.

Liam rolled off the bed and grabbed the mobile from his pocket.

'Yeah, we're fine. Okay. Slow down. Look, we got caught. We've just been hiding out at the hut. Jesus, okay, Dad.' Liam ended the call. 'We'd better get back there or they're coming to look for us.'

* * *

'I still don't understand. Where are your other clothes?' Lizzie questioned on the drive back in the cab of the truck. 'Wait, did something happen between you two?'

Angie glanced across at Liam and pursed her lips together. How could she get away with what they'd done when she looked so guilty?

'Did you two *do it*?'

'No!' Angie snapped. 'Of course nothing happened.'

'Then where are your other clothes?' Lizzie was relentless in her line of questioning, but Angie wasn't going to give in, at least while Liam was still in the truck.

When they finally reached the farm, Angie and Liam received sideways glances from everyone, even the old man.

Instead of letting their judging eyes to embarrass her, Angie wished she had the time to pull Liam into a bush and go all the way with him. Something had kick-started her heart. After so many years of zero intimacy, she wasn't going about life on autopilot anymore. Everything seemed to have more colour. More vibrancy. Life seemed a little less serious.

When it was time to say goodbye, Angie waited by the car.

'Can we go home now? Or do you need to say goodbye to your lover?'

'Lizzie, we need to thank them for their hospitality.'

'I don't need to thank them for anything, All I got was burnt shoulders and a rash between my legs,' Lizzie muttered under her breath.

After letting the final horse into the paddock, Liam headed over to the Honda. The tracksuit he was wearing looked equally ridiculous as hers, though on him it was still somehow sexy.

'Time to go?' he asked when he reached the car and leaned against the bonnet.

'I wish it wasn't.'

The rain had cleared and the sky was now a beautiful blue. It brought a smile to her face.

Liam took her hands in his. 'I'm sorry it's over for today.'

'Me too.' Her heart squeezed a little at the thought of leaving.

'When're you coming back to Canberra?'

Liam smiled, still holding onto her hands. 'Is that an invitation?'

'Maybe.'

'How about you give me your phone.'

Angie leaned into the car and rummaged through her handbag. She handed him the sleek device and watched him type something.

He handed it back to her with a smile.

'What's this?' she asked when she looked at the screen of her phone.

'My number.'

Now she really wanted to pull him behind the bushes and have her way with him.

'If you ever want to catch up, you know where to find me. Call me anytime. I get back to Canberra on Monday morning.' Liam leaned in to kiss her on the cheek.

At the last minute, Angie turned her face towards him and their lips met. There was no way she was going to miss out on one last kiss from this cowboy.

'Cheeky girl,' he whispered in her ear as he embraced her in a hug. 'Maybe we can finish what we started back in Canberra.'

'I'd like that.'

'And I hope you don't still think this is the worst birthday yet.' His whispers were turning her insides upside down.

'I don't think it would be fair to say it was the *worst* birthday.'

'I hope I had something to do with that.'

Liam may have been three years younger, but he was pure Australian muscle and Angie hoped there was something more between them than just basic, animalistic attraction.

She grabbed his hands and pulled them around her waist, letting them fall in the curve of her back.

She stood on her tippy toes and whispered in his ear 'I can say without a doubt this is the best birthday I've ever had.'

BIRTHDAY BOY

Book two

FATE BROUGHT THEM TOGETHER. WILL REALITY TEAR THEM APART?

CHAPTER ONE

The phone almost slipped through Angie's fingers.

'What do you mean you're not coming home? I'm at the Canberra airport. Your flight was meant to arrive twenty minutes ago,' she said as she glared at the digital watch on her wrist.

'I'm in Hawaii.'

The words slapped across her face like the dry heat of summer air.

'Hawaii?' None of it made sense to Angie. Her husband was meant to be waiting at the airport with his luggage at four o'clock sharp.

'Was there a delay with the flight? Is that why you're not here?'

'Look, there's no easy way to say this, Angie. I met someone.'

Angie clutched at her chest as the flurry of people moved in and out of the airport. Some hugged their loved ones, some kissed, some even cried. It was Christmas time. Of course families were hugging their loved ones. It was what people did at this time of year. Yet instead of seeing her husband for the first time in two weeks, she'd been stood up.

A spark of heat struck Angie's collarbone and shot up her neck to her cheeks. It was happening again. All over again.

Craig had broken her heart and crushed her soul only a few years earlier when he dumped her on her birthday and revealed his mistress was pregnant. And now, another cheating scumbag had reared his ugly head and she was paying the price.

He met someone.

'What the fuck, Michael?' It was all she could muster in the moment.

The people hugging their loved ones stopped their chatter and turned to stare. Their critical eyes were the last thing Angie cared about.

She'd married Michael only two months earlier. They were still in the honeymoon phase. Still on the trend of having sex twice a day, mornings of post-coital bliss. Now he was telling her he'd met someone else?

'Angie, I'm sorry. Maybe we rushed into things too soon.' His voice crackled over the phone.

Angie pressed the phone closer to her ear.

'Coming over here has given me some time to think. A lot of time.'

'And perhaps some time screw around with someone else who isn't your wife!'

'Angie, come on.'

'Come on? Really, Michael? You said a minute ago it was too soon for us. It's a bit late to tell me this, don't you think? I've already changed my last name and altered all my identity documents. Do you know how much grief it is to get a new passport? A new licence? Do you know how much our wedding cost! My dress was a one-off, hand-made lace piece from Italy I'll never get to wear again.' Heat sparked through her chest again and it was becoming harder to breathe.

'Why do you care how much the wedding cost? *You* didn't even pay for it.'

Angie drew in a sharp breath. The cost of their wedding wasn't the point. Being married was all Angie had wanted for so long. She'd wanted a husband, to start a family. Someone to stand by her side and alleviate the loneliness of this ugly, cruel world when it all became too much.

'You cheated on me after two months of marriage. How could you do this to me?'

He didn't answer the question.

'And don't you dare try and turn this around on me and act like those vows meant nothing. Is there more than one, Michael? How many others have you screwed while we've been together?' Angie was well aware Michael was entitled and arrogant. According to him, he deserved *all* the good things in life. And when he wanted something, he chased it relentlessly. It was why Angie had married him. Michael had chased her, wooed her, until he got what he wanted. And now she was left to pick up the pieces of their broken relationship.

'We're supposed to be spending a week at Gumtree Plains in the Snowy Mountains. I rented a holiday house and we leave tonight. Am I supposed to cancel the booking?'

'I don't know, go up with there with Lizzie and have a girl's weekend.'

'At Christmas? She's got her own family and responsibilities, I can't ask her to drop everything for me. You, on the other hand—'

'Angie, look. We're over, I'm sorry.' He paused. 'I'll reimburse you for the booking.'

Angie clenched her fist.

How dare he.

This wasn't some business transaction he could throw money at to fix.

'This is supposed to be our first Christmas together as a married couple. We didn't get a proper honeymoon because of your work schedule. *I* need this holiday.' She loved her job. It was what got her out of bed each morning and gave her life purpose. But even Angie wasn't immune to the inevitable burnout resulting from the long-hours and demands of being a solicitor.

She was met with silence.

'Look, Angie, I have to go. I'm sorry, I didn't mean to hurt you. My lawyers are drafting up papers for the property settlement and divorce.' He ended the call.

That was it? After two months of marriage, that's all he had to say. He wasn't even going to try?

She pressed the call button again and waited for him to pick up. It went straight to voicemail.

Angie couldn't contain the sizzling heat rising in her chest. She flung the smartphone across the airport with all her strength. It connected with the shiny white tiles and slid across the surface.

'Ma'am. Is everything alright?'

Angie looked over her shoulder as tears bubbled in her eyes.

A stranger in a red airline uniform stood there with her hands behind her back. The woman's perfect blonde hair was pulled back in a slick ponytail. Her neatly pressed shirt and pencil skirt forced Angie's inferiority complex to rise from the ashes.

'No, not really. I'll survive though. Sorry about my little… tantrum.'

As if this perfect stranger cared about her personal problems.

'I'll show myself out.' Angie grabbed the smartphone off the tiles, noting the crack down the screen

A reflection of my life.

As Angie walked back to the car in the sweltering summer heat, her pencil thin heels rubbed against her ankles. She had two weeks off work. Two weeks to think about how her husband had left her and had already jumped into bed with someone else.

Fuck.

How the hell was she going to explain this to her family? Her colleagues?

The truth was she'd rather be at work now. Work was what she lived for. She was at her best in the court room. Fighting for the rights of her clients. Justice needed to be served by someone. So why did she want to lie in front of the television, eat ice cream and sob away her aching heart?

She couldn't stand it anymore. Stopping in the middle of the footpath, she lifted her leg and pulled off the sky-high heel. Once she pulled the other shoe off, she briskly walked back to the car, trying to keep her bare feet off the hot concrete.

When she made it back to the car, the cracked phone rang in her hand.

'Well, hello lovers. How was the trip, Mikey? Did you get to do a Baywatch run like the show? Please tell me you met some hot male lifeguards.'

'It's just me, Lizzie,' Angie said as she pulled herself into the front seat of the car.

'Oh. Sorry. Michael not with you?'

Angie was silent as she settled into the driver seat of the new Mercedes. It was a wedding gift from Michael. Purchasing a car with a luxury tax wasn't where Angie liked to put her savings, but she certainly wasn't going to say no when she arrived at the dealership and it was sitting in the display room with a red bow on the bonnet.

'Nope.'

'Where is he? You left work early to pick him up.'

Angie pressed the start button of the car to let the air conditioning circulate. 'He's still in Hawaii because apparently, he met someone else.'

'Uh...someone else?' Lizzie's words hung in the air.

'Yes. Someone else.' Angie couldn't think who it could be. Maybe it was someone she knew. Maybe it was a younger babe he'd met on the beach. This whole revelation made her question whether she knew Michael at all.

Her stomach clenched. How could she have gotten it so wrong? She grabbed her tummy and pressed her head into the steering wheel as the air conditioning circulated through the car.

'Shit, Ange. I'm so sorry. I feel terrible. I should never have set you guys up on a blind date.'

'Lizzie it's not your fault,' Angie replied through tears.

Her husband had met someone else. Even if he didn't change his mind, could she stay with him knowing he'd cheated?

It's what all the men in her life did. The vows they exchanged obviously meant nothing to him.

'So, what's going to happen?' Lizzie asked.

Angie closed her eyes and sighed. 'I guess I'm getting divorced.'

CHAPTER TWO

The church doors swung open and a gust of summer wind blew into his face.

Liam breathed in the divine warm air and jogged down the steps of the church, pulling off his tie and unbuttoning the top button on the collar of his shirt.

It'd taken all his strength to not protest when the priest asked for those with objections to speak up or forever hold their peace.

It wouldn't have been fair to speak up and air his dirty laundry. Mum would've killed him for disrespecting the sanctity of marriage, especially under God's eye in a church. And besides, Bec knew how he felt, yet she'd still gone through with the wedding. It was probably a bad idea to accept and invitation to the nuptials of his ex- girlfriend to his ex-best mate.

'Liam!'

Liam stopped on the bottom step of the church. The sound of her voice was so sweet, like the soft strumming of a classical guitar. He didn't want to turn around and face the raw betrayal of her actions, even though they'd been broken up for three years.

'I'd love it if you could stay,' Bec said, almost in a whisper.

Liam turned on his boots and stared up the stairs.

Bec, his high school sweetheart, stood at the entrance of the church, wearing a white princess ballgown. The long veil flew softly with the wind and the sun shone down, highlighting the tiara carefully placed in her long, curled auburn hair.

The sight of her tugged at his heart. Was it meant to be him standing next to her at the altar in his best tuxedo?

Now he'd never know.

I'm just an unwelcome guest in an ill-fitting suit.

He was nobody. Unimportant. Love didn't live in his heart anymore. Only regret.

'Thanks for inviting me to the wedding, Bec, but I've got things to do today,' Liam said as he turned to make his way to the carpark.

'Liam,' she pleaded as she took another step down the stairs. 'We're friends and I want you to celebrate this with us.'

Liam stopped and turned around. The feeling wasn't mutual. If it wasn't for Mum, he wouldn't have even gone to the bloody ceremony.

Like I want to watch my ex-girlfriend marry someone else.

'Bec, don't make this any harder than it has to be, okay. Whatever we had, it's over.

Nothing gained, nothing lost. I wish you all the best. Both of you. But I can't stand here and pretend what happened was right.' He turned on his heels and jogged to his ute.

As the wind whipped his cheeks, he kept the tears in check. Running away from Bec was the only way he could stop himself from crumbling completely onto the gravel road.

* * *

'Your Mum said you were at a wedding today. What're you doing here then?'

'Come on, Grandad. You know exactly why I didn't hang around,' Liam said as he stepped inside the cottage and took off his suit jacket.

He kicked off his boots and left them at the front door, the way Grandma taught him as a young boy. Tugging at the tie, he pulled it over his head and hung it on the coat rack.

Grandad stood in the kitchen of the old cottage, hunched over a steaming mug of coffee as he stirred through milk and sugar.

'Your first love. Boy, you never get over that one. How did she look in the dress?'

Liam slumped into the old, leather sofa and ran a shaking hand through his thick hair. If he could go back to this morning, he would've put up a better argument with Mum to not go at all. 'More beautiful than I could've ever imagined,' he said after a long, drawn out sigh.

'Well, what's it your Grandma used to say? Plenty of seahorses in the ocean?'

Liam smiled at Grandad's poor memory. 'Fish in the sea, Grandad. Same thing, I guess,' Liam said, trying to hold back a laugh.

Grandad shrugged and brought the cup of coffee over to the lounge. He placed it on a coaster on the coffee table and took a seat in the brown leather armchair. That chair was famous now after being in the cottage since it was built, over one hundred years ago.

'What, no coffee for me?'

'You know where to find it, boy. I'm not your mother.'

Same stubbornness, even at ninety.

'You'll get over what's-her-name,' Grandad said with a wave of his hand after he took a sip of the coffee. 'I'm still not over losing your Grandma, but our love was different. We were married longer than some people live! Soul mates, her and I. How long were we together again?'

'Sixty-two years,' Liam confirmed.

Grandad tried to do the calculation in his head as he counted with his fingers. 'Geez, that's a bloody long time.' After a moment he slumped back into the armchair. He glanced over at the framed photo of him and his wife on their wedding day, sitting proudly above the dusty piano.

Liam glanced at Grandad and noticed a tear pop in the corner of his eye. Their love was unlike anything he'd seen. Even though they bickered non-stop, there was a lot of love between his grandparents.

'Never mind. She's better off where she is. No more pain from that damn cancer,' Grandad finally said before sipping his coffee.

'That's right.'

'You'll be okay. You're a strong boy. Always have been.'

Liam pressed his back into the soft leather. 'I know, Grandad. It's not like I'm going to die. But, I....' he paused before saying the words. 'I can't stop wondering whether it was meant to be me standing up there today.'

Grandad nodded slowly, but didn't respond. The silence between them allowed the ticking of the grandfather clock to take Liam's focus.

'I like to think of these things as an opportunity. There's something waiting for you round the corner. Someone you're meant to be with. I can feel it in my bones.'

'Feel it in your bones? Are you sure it's not your arthritis?'

Grandad glared at Liam. 'Bugger off.'

After a few moments, Liam stood up and walked to the kitchen to make his own cup of coffee.

'Grandad, you want a biscuit?'

Silence.

'Grandad?'

A snort perforated through the cottage. The old man always fell asleep at the most inappropriate times.

Liam didn't want to be alone with his thoughts. Not today.

Maybe he wasn't the great boyfriend he always thought himself to be. Maybe he should've travelled with Bec when she wanted to explore the world.

Liam had other aspirations though. A career. A new life in Canberra. Backpacking wasn't his idea of a holiday. Now he was questioning every decision he'd ever made, wondering if it was all one big mistake.

He dropped two teaspoons of coffee into the mug and poured in boiling water from the kettle.

When Bec told Liam's ex-best mate, Damo, she was going overseas, Damo jumped at the chance to be her companion.

While stirring the coffee, Liam remembered reading the text message. Of course he was uncomfortable Damo had decided to go overseas with her. Damo always did have a thing for Bec. They both showed their true colours when they came back as a couple. And just like that, three years ago, the woman he thought he was supposed to spend the rest of his life with, fell into the arms of another man.

Liam took the mug to the lounge and sat down on the sofa. He took a large gulp of the boiling coffee.

'Christ,' he spat, as the boiling liquid travelled down his throat.

Pay attention, numnuts.

Liam placed the mug on a coaster to let it cool down, and sat back in the leather couch. Maybe he wasn't destined to marry Bec. It'd been years since they'd dated, and as far as he was concerned, he'd moved on.

But weddings had a way of bringing out the worst in people.

CHAPTER THREE

'Angie, what're you doing?'

Angie drew a sharp breath as she jolted awake from a hazy dream in the middle of the king size bed. When she looked around, she was covered in designer clothes Michael had bought for her during their relationship. Clothes she'd strewn across the bedroom in a fit of rage when she'd arrived home hours earlier.

'Oh hun, you look like you've been crying?'

'No I don't.' She dismissed Lizzie's suggestion as she furiously wiped her eyes in an attempt to erase any trace of emotion.

Lizzie cocked her brow and pulled a mirror from her purse. She held it in front of Angie. The reflection wasn't her own.

Fucking panda eyes!

'I'm a little upset, okay. My prick of a husband cheated on me and left me in the dust while he's living it up with some beach babe in Hawaii.'

'It doesn't explain why you've removed your entire wardrobe and thrown it across the bedroom floor.'

Admittedly, the room was a mess. Was she having a mental break down? The last thing she remembered was storming into the penthouse, rushing to the walk-in robe and screaming as she threw her clothes around the room.

The sight of the mess made her throat constrict. It was almost an exact replica of her apartment after she'd found out Craig had cheated.

I guess I can count myself a professional at being dumped.

Angie glanced up at Lizzie as the tears began to fall once more. 'What is it about me that makes men cheat and leave me for other women?' The question was raw, almost too raw for Angie to handle.

She picked up her wedding dress and sobbed into the material.

'No, no, no,' Lizzie said as she dropped her handbag on the bedroom floor and climbed onto the bed with Angie. 'Your husband is a jackass, you hear me? *You* are not the problem. If he can't see what an amazing person you are, that's his God damned loss. He *will* regret this and come crawling back. I have no doubt.'

'What, so I can be his sloppy seconds? I don't know what the hell to do now. I took a vow that I would be loyal for life. They meant something to me.'

Lizzie pulled away from Angie. Angie's face was wet from tears. Lizzie grabbed the wedding dress and raised it to Angie's face to wipe the tears away.

'You *will* get through this. And then we'll trash this designer dress in spectacular style in a cleansing ceremony. Throw paint on it and watch it burn as we drink bubbly and laugh about what a total loser he is. We'll even take photos and send them to him, just for kicks.'

The comment made Angie laugh, but only for a moment. Deep in her heart, she knew their relationship was doomed from the start. Everyone told her marrying Michael was a bad idea. Lizzie had reservations. Even Mum, who'd imagined her daughter's wedding from the moment she was born, told Angie she shouldn't go through with it.

When she looked back on it now, who would? They'd mixed in the same circles for over twelve months, but only dated for three months before Michael got down on one knee and flashed the biggest diamond ring Angie had ever seen.

No one could deny she'd been swept off her feet by Michael, and the finer things in life he was able to provide. At face value, marrying Michael was like winning the lottery ticket in love.

The IT entrepreneur from a wealthy family spent most of his time travelling the world. He was everything, and more, Angie could've dreamed of. Except now, she was dealing with the fallout of an impending divorce.

No!

This couldn't be happening. Angie could *not* be a divorcee before thirty. The only thing working in her favour was managing other people's divorces for a living.

'Do you want me to stay the night?'

Angie shook her head. 'No, you have a date.'

'Please, we matched on a dating app. I can ditch the loser. You're way more important than some dude who'll probably just stare at my boobs all night.'

Lizzie's crass comment brought a smile to Angie's face.

'Look, a smile. My sense of humour hasn't failed me.'

'I want you to go on your date,' Angie said as she sniffled and wiped her nose on the wedding dress. 'I'm heading to Gumtree Plains anyway.'

'Tonight?' Lizzie looked around at the mess in the room. 'Are you sure that's a good idea? You seem a little…not yourself.'

Angie glanced over the bed. Broken glass covered the carpet from a frame she'd broken earlier when she ran into the room in a rage.

An exact replica of my life. What the hell have I become?

'Driving in your state? I don't know if you should right now.'

'It's fine. All I need to do is have a shower and clean up. No point wasting a night's accommodation fees.'

The truth was, Angie didn't want to stay in the penthouse. A house of lies. The beautiful wedding photos strategically placed in each room, seemed like they belonged to someone else now. She was an imposter in a random's apartment.

'If you need to stop along the way and call me, do it. You don't have to do this alone.'

'Thanks for the offer,' Angie said as she moved off the bed and grabbed a suitcase from the walk-in wardrobe. 'But the most dramatic thing that could've happened has already gone down. I can't imagine this day getting any worse.'

* * *

The music was turned up as loud as her ears could handle. It was the ultimate breakup mix tape; the playlist she created when crusty Craig broke her heart the first time around. Pelting out the high notes was liberating and the weight on her chest was slowly lifting.

According to the GPS, she was only twenty minutes from her destination. The road was pitch black and rain plummeted down as she rounded crests and curves on the country road towards Gumtree Plains.

With the lights on high beam, it was like driving in a tunnel. She'd never been a fan of night driving, but couldn't spend a second longer in Michael's penthouse. Even when she left, it was as if the walls were closing in, suffocating her until she could no longer breathe.

Headlights in the distance behind her shone brightly as they got closer. Seconds later, a ute appeared. The speed limit was one hundred kilometres, but she was doing eighty. Driving to the conditions was a must, especially in the country.

She turned the windscreen wipers up a notch as the rain pelted down in large drops on the windscreen. The ute behind beeped and began swerving across the line onto the other side of the road.

'What are you, drunk? Go around.' Angie stared into the rear-view mirror and signalled for them to overtake.

They didn't take the hint. The horn blasted again. This time Angie pulled off to the left and the ute overtook. The driver held the horn and screamed obscenities out the window.

As quickly as the ute arrived, it disappeared into the distance, leaving her alone in the darkness of the night.

'Bloody morons.' Angie pulled back out onto the road and accelerated to eighty.

Some people don't get it.

She settled into a comfortable speed and continued the journey. Out of the corner of her eye, something moved in the bushes amongst the trees. Before she had time to react, a kangaroo jumped into the middle of the road.

She slammed the brakes. The wheels jarred as they locked and slid across the black tar.

The kangaroo's eyes locked onto hers and widened under the bright lights coming towards it.

Angie squeezed her eyes shut and screamed as the car collided with the animal, and her head flung forward and smashed against the steering wheel.

CHAPTER FOUR

His eyes opened to a dark room. Not even a sliver of light trickled through the corners of the windows.

It had to be past nine. There was a slight chill in the air, peculiar for the middle of summer in Gumtree Plains.

A yawn escaped his lips as Liam sat up on the old leather couch. Craning his neck to the side, he glanced at the grandfather clock. It was almost nine thirty.

Shit. Grandad's medication.

Liam pushed himself off the couch and headed towards the kitchen to check on Grandad's Webster pack.

'Who the hell are you?'

Liam's body jolted and he turned around. The hallway light was on and the old man was wearing flannelette pyjamas as he shuffled towards the kitchen.

'Grandad. It's me, Liam.'

The old man stepped closer and looked him up and down with a critical eye. 'Who're you calling an old man? I'm as fit as a fiddle.'

Liam put his hands on his hips and stared at Grandad. 'You're not getting out of taking your medication.'

The old man huffed as he pushed past Liam into the kitchen. 'It's a conspiracy. I don't need medication. The government's trying to brainwash me,' he grumbled as he filled a glass of water at the sink.

The first rule of dementia was to not try and convince the person with dementia they had the disease. It was only the early stages. A few forgetful things here and there. Liam had noticed it progressively getting worse. He wanted to maintain Grandad's dignity, so he played along when Grandad dug in his heels about the medication.

'Think of it this way, Grandad. If you take your pills, you'll continue to be as fit as a fiddle. It's a preventative, to keep your brain and your bones working their best.' Liam patted Grandad's shoulder.

The old man softened and put his hand on Liam's. 'Alright, if you insist. But only because you're my favourite grandson.' He popped the pills in his mouth and washed them down with a glass of water.

Liam laughed. 'I'm pretty sure you're not allowed to say that. Harry would be devastated.'

'I'm old, I can say whatever I like. Now, you'd best go home because I need my beauty sleep.'

Grandad turned and hobbled down the hallway back to bed.

Liam called out, 'Don't worry, Grandad. I'll see myself out.' He grabbed the tie and suit jacket from the coat rack, pulled on his boots and stepped outside.

A gust of wind rushed into the house from the storm swirling outside. As Liam prepared to make a run to the ute, his phone buzzed in his pocket. When he pulled it out, there was a message from his mate, Jaxon.

I'm still waiting for your answer. Don't you want to get out of your dead-end economics job and come start a bar with me? You know it'll be the best decision you'll ever make.

Liam pushed the phone back into his pocket and jogged to the ute. He wasn't in the right state of mind to think about starting up a bar with his mate.

Not tonight.

* * *

Since he'd bailed on the wedding and wasn't up for cooking, the only place with food available at this time of night was the Gumtree Plains Pub. After watching his ex-girlfriend marry his ex-best friend and sleeping through most of the evening, there was only one option. A burger and chips.

He turned the keys in the ignition of the old ute. The engine grumbled before kickstarting to life. Liam always drove one of the old utes from home when he was visiting. The kangaroos in Gumtree Plains were bigger and badder, and a bull bar would at least provide some protection if he collided with one.

The rain fell down to earth and Liam flicked on the windscreen wipers to get a clear vision of the road. The wipers slowly smeared the rain from one side to the other. The steering wheel moved easily under his expert hands as he accelerated away from the cottage, past the house and up to the main road.

When the ute hit the bitumen, the rain started to fall heavily, so he flicked the windscreen wipers onto the highest setting. They were no match for mother nature and left smudge marks across the glass.

As Liam rounded Hellfire Bend, the second last turn before town, he spotted high beam lights over the hill. He flashed once to tell the other driver to turn them off. The attempt failed.

As he neared, he realised the other car wasn't moving. When the ute made it over the crest, he could see the car had stopped on the opposite side of the road. It was black, so it was hard to make out the shape. But the dead kangaroo in front of it was a giveaway of what had happened.

Shit.

When he reached the car, Liam steered the ute off the side of the road. After he pulled up the handbrake, he jumped outside into the blistering rain. For a hot summer night, the rain sure had a frosty bite to it, nipping at the exposed skin on his forearms where he'd rolled up the sleeves of his shirt.

'Hello?' He called out. 'Are you okay?'

It was a woman in the driver seat. Her head was pressed against the steering wheel.

'Hello?' Liam ran up to the window and banged against it with his fist. For a moment the woman was lifeless. Then she seemed to rise from the dead. Taking a large gulp of air, she sat up straight and stared ahead, letting her eyes adjust.

She looked around the car, clearly disoriented. When she turned to Liam, he stepped backwards into the middle of the road as he clasped his chest.

'Angie?'

What the hell was she doing back in Gumtree Plains? It'd been over eight months since he'd last seen her. Not that he was counting.

She never called me.

An ear-piercing scream escaped Angie's lungs. Liam rushed back to the driver door and tried to open it. It was locked.

Angie pushed the car door open, almost colliding with Liam's groin. She slid out of the Mercedes and got to her feet.

Liam's heart pounded in his chest when he noticed the light blue denim shorts and baggy white t-shirt clinging to her petite frame. As the rain wet her clothes, they clung to her skin and showed off every curve. Curves he'd never forgotten.

She stumbled to the front of her car, supporting herself on the black bonnet. 'What the...what happened to my—' she stopped when she spotted the kangaroo lying in in the middle of the road. 'Jesus, I killed it!'

The wail pierced Liam's heart. She began to sob while the rain penetrated her clothes.

'It's going to be okay, right?'

Had she recognized him?

Liam's memory was crystal clear. The rain pelting down to earth, saturating her clothes

and short blonde hair, forced back memories of the hut and the afternoon they'd spent together, intertwined in each other's arms. A day, despite trying to forget it, he never managed to erase from his memory.

'It could be stunned,' he lied. 'I think you need to go to the hospital. You might have a concussion,' he said after spotting a bruise on her head.

'We need to help the kangaroo,' she cried through the torrential rain.

'It's pouring and we're on a bend in the road. It's too dangerous for us to stay here.'

How could he tell her the kangaroo couldn't be saved? Instead, he attempted the practical route.

'Come on, hop into the ute. We need to get out of this storm.'

Angie didn't move. She stood in the headlights, staring at the lifeless kangaroo. He couldn't wait any longer. They were either going to get hit by an unsuspecting driver, or one of them would catch pneumonia from the storm. Neither were chances Liam was willing to take.

He sprinted to the Mercedes and took the keys from the ignition. Then he grabbed Angie's hand and led her across the road to the ute. He opened the door and encouraged her into the passenger seat.

As Angie grabbed the handle and pulled herself into the car, Liam's nose was assaulted by her sweet perfume.

This isn't the time or the place to feel some kind of way about this woman.

He ran to the driver side and pulled himself in.

'I'm taking you to the hospital.'

'No.' The demanding tone in her voice made Liam stop and think before defying her again.

'You've hit your head on the steering wheel. And by the looks of it, you had a pretty big prang with a roo.'

'Don't you dare take me to the hospital,' she growled. 'I'm here for a holiday and I refuse to sit in a waiting area for hours on end only to be told to go home and rest. I'm fine.'

'Okay,' Liam replied, backing down. 'Where can I take you then?'

'Gumtree Lakehouse.'

Liam knew where the house was. It was one of the best holiday homes in the Snowy Mountains, and was famous for bringing tourists to the area.

He stole one last glance at Angie before turning the ute around and hitting the accelerator.

CHAPTER FIVE

The kangaroo. That poor kangaroo. Is it dead? It must be dead.

Now she'd had a moment to think about it she hoped it had passed away, but only because she didn't want it to suffer. The vision of the kangaroo's terrified eyes kept circling in her mind.

Finally, when she'd calmed herself down, she looked around, not recognising the vehicle she was sitting in.

She swallowed. Hard. Angie didn't normally take lifts with strangers. In her line of work, she'd seen a lot of dodgy people, particularly opportunistic men who'd take advantage of a lone woman the first chance they got. But still being in shock from the accident, she didn't really have another choice.

It's not like my bloody husband will come and rescue me.

Without looking at the man, she asked, 'Can I drive my car?'

'The important thing is you're okay. Are you sure I can't take you to the hospital?'

'No hospital.' Angie was adamant. Sure, her head throbbed like it'd been hit with a brick, but there was no way her husband was going to get a holiday in Hawaii with some beautiful stranger, while she sat in a sterile waiting room at the hospital a week before Christmas with a concussion. No. She'd go to this holiday house and have a great time, whatever the cost.

The ute pulled up in a narrow driveway and passed an old wooden sign that read: *Gumtree Lakehouse. Where the view can't be beaten.* It swung with the gale force wind of the storm.

'Here we are.'

It was hard to see in the dark, though she managed to make out the shape of the house. The ad on the internet advertised it as a split-level home. Four bedrooms, an ensuite, separate bath. Large entertaining spaces. A balcony overlooking the lake.

Angie opened the passenger door and stumbled to the front door, tripping over her own feet as the rain persisted. She didn't want to admit she was a little dizzy from the accident and her throbbing head had given her vertigo.

The man walked up behind her. He leaned down to the welcome mat and pulled a key from underneath.

'You know this place?'

'Everyone around here knows this place. It's famous with the tourists,' he said as he shoved the key into the lock and opened the door.

The door swung open and Angie searched for the light switch by patting her hand across the wall. When she finally found the switch, she flicked it on.

The lights lit up the entire house, revealing a quaint getaway. Even in her possibly concussed state, Angie was impressed by the size and space of the house. The open living room transitioned into the kitchen, and then dining area. At the end of the living space was a balcony with gum trees for privacy. Stairs led to the bottom floor, where the bedrooms were located.

As she walked through the top floor, she noticed glass all around. Looking through the glass, out over the balcony, she could make out a still, dark lake.

When she turned around, she stared at the handsome stranger. Familiarity struck. And then a moment later, she remembered.

'Liam?'

'Hey,' he replied with an awkward wave.

Her heart began to thud in her chest and thoughts of the day in the hut flooded back. Their skin touching. His lips. Tongue. Warmth washed over her body in a way Michael had never triggered. The sweet sensation Liam helped her release that day made her yearn for his touch all over again. And God, he was so sexy in the rain-drenched, long-sleeved white shirt rolled up to his elbows.

In different circumstances, she might've grabbed the tie hanging around his neck and pulled him towards her, kissing him impatiently and taking the afternoon in the hut one step further.

'Are you okay?' Liam asked.

Angie ran her trembling hands down her arms where goose bumps had risen on her skin. 'Yeah, fine. But I have no clothes or food and...' she looked around the house.

It was strange, knowing she'd be staying in this huge house all alone with nothing but her thoughts. While she needed a break from the penthouse in Canberra, she didn't know if she was ready to face whatever crazy thoughts were hiding in the darkest places of her mind.

'Will you be alright if I leave you alone for twenty minutes?'

'I guess so,' she replied, hoping the throbbing in her head was nothing more than a headache.

Liam stepped out of the house and closed the door behind him.

Reality settled in. She was standing in a huge house, in a place she didn't know, alone with nothing but her crazy thoughts.

* * *

Steam from the long shower covered the mirror above the basin in the ensuite.

Angie wiped her hand over the foggy mirror to get a better look at the reflection. A bruise was shaping up nicely in the middle of her forehead where she'd collided with the steering wheel. She leaned forward and touched it with her index finger.

'Ouch,' she muttered.

It was fresh. All too fresh. Not only had her husband admitted to cheating and announced he was leaving her, she was now sporting a fresh bruise that made her look like she'd come off second best in a boxing match.

The realisation she was about to separate from her husband sent her heartbeat into a flurry, the thudding so loud it vibrated in her ears.

She grabbed a towel from the rack and wrapped it around her body. How was it fair that the men who cheated and betrayed her always ended up with a happy, perfect life?

After each break up, her exes moved on with someone else at lightning speed. To them, she was nothing more than the garbage they threw away on bin day. And it made her wonder, *is there something wrong with me?*

The doorbell rang. Angie jogged upstairs in a towel and her hair dripping at the ends. When she opened the door, it was Liam.

She froze.

It wasn't a dream. It was plausible in her state she was imaging things. But Liam was real. The man she'd longed over for eight months was now standing on her porch.

'I brought food. And I got some things from your car too. Your handbag and a bag of clothes were in the back.' Liam dropped the handbag and clothes at the door and handed the boxes of pizza to Angie.

There he was, standing in a dress shirt with several buttons undone, and a loose tie hanging around his neck. Seeing him now forced her to acknowledge her mistake.

Michael may have had it all, but he didn't give Angie what she needed. He didn't even try. Maybe if she'd given Liam a chance, things might've turned out differently.

'Thanks. I'm kinda—' Angie looked down at the short towel barely covering her thighs.

Liam's eyes travelled up her body. 'Sorry, how rude of me. I was leaving anyway. I thought it'd be good for you to have some food. Didn't want you going to bed on an empty stomach, especially after the night you've had.' Liam placed the pizza boxes on a nearby coffee table, and turned to leave.

'Wait!' Angie called out as she followed Liam out onto the front porch. The storm had subsided to a pleasantly light mist.

'I can't eat two pizzas on my own and it seems like a waste to throw the other one away. Perhaps you could stay for dinner?'

CHAPTER SIX

Liam sat at the glass dining table observing the interior of the house. Angie had changed into dry clothes and was now serving the pizza onto plates at the dining table.

It was hard to forget what happened between them. An afternoon of passion. But then she never called him.

Now she was serving pizza like they were old friends catching up.

'There you go,' she said as she placed a plate in front of him.

The pizza was probably cold, but that didn't curb his hunger.

'So, you're back in the mountains. What convinced you to come back?' His eyes connected with Angie's, searching for a reason why she would come back when she had no apparent connection to this place.

She smiled, although it didn't reach her eyes. Was it insincere, or was something else on her mind?

'I needed a holiday and some fresh air. Couldn't think of a better place,' she said as she sat down at the dining table.

'Not Bali or Fiji? The weather would be tops in December.'

Angie took a bite of pizza. 'School holidays are a nightmare at this time of year. Destination holidays turn kids into rude little monsters.'

Liam could only imagine. They could be rude little monsters at the best of times. 'How've you been, other than planning a holiday?'

She waved her hand in the air as if to signal things couldn't be better. Then Liam spotted her left hand and the glitzy diamond ring. Angie caught his eye and placed it on her lap, under the table.

'I've been working. Not much else to tell. I live a pretty uneventful life back in Canberra.'

Then why does it feel like you're lying?

Liam had no right to ask questions or pry into her life. He certainly wasn't going to push her for an answer as to why she never called. She didn't owe him anything. It was an afternoon of fun, and he was happy to leave it at that.

Even I don't believe that.

While the breakup and betrayal by Bec had torn his heart apart at first, he knew he had to move on for his own sanity, especially after he found out about her impending nuptials over a year ago. It was at that point he finally accepted Bec was an ex for a reason.

Bec was a convenient choice for his future, but that didn't mean she was the one. And the afternoon in the hut with Angie proved Bec wasn't right for him in many ways.

There was something about Angie that drew him in. Something about her made him want her more.

'And what about you?' Angie asked.

Liam pulled the crust off the pizza. 'Oh same. Working to pay the bills back in Canberra.'

'What do you do for work?'

'I work at an economics firm in Canberra. I'm an adviser.'

'An economist?'

'Yeah, I did economics at uni, so it seemed like the next logical step.'

'Good with numbers then, unlike me,' Angie replied with a smile.

By this point, most women had lost interest in hearing about what he did for work. There was no way to make his job sound sexy. And if he had it his way, he'd already be running a bar with his friend Jax.

'It's not forever. It's just a paycheque at the moment. I'm actually thinking of investing in a bar with my mate.'

'Sounds like fun. If you can follow your dreams, you should do it. We only live once. May as well make the most of it.'

There was silence as they nibbled mindlessly on the pizza. Liam noticed the bruise on Angie's head starting to turn purple.

Angie stopped eating and dropped a slice of pizza on her plate.

'I'm sorry, Liam. I've lost my appetite. I think I should go to bed. I've had a pretty stressful day.'

'Of course.'

My cue to leave.

Liam stood and took their plates to the sink. After he rinsed and popped them into the dishwasher, he headed for the front door.

'Liam?'

Even the sound of her voice sent chills across his skin. He turned around, hoping she'd changed her mind and might ask him to stay a little longer.

'What's going to happen to my car?'

Liam's shoulders slumped slightly. 'I know someone who can take a look at it in the morning. Goodnight.'

* * *

'Well, there's some pretty serious damage. I'm going to need to keep it here for at least two weeks. With the Christmas holidays, business has been crazy.'

It wasn't good news. Angie had come to Gumtree Plains for a holiday and now she had no transport.

'Is it a write-off?'

'Nah, it'll be fine. Whoever owns this baby will be spending a pretty penny to get her fixed though. Hope the owner has insurance.'

The mechanic shop was abuzz with activity. For a small town, business was booming. Chatter was in the air as clients entered and left the office. Oil covered the concrete floors and the radio's music blared in the background.

Men were hoisting cars up to the ceiling to get a better look underneath. Angie's car didn't seem nearly as out of place with the front crumpled in like the other damaged cars sitting lifeless around in the shop. Though it was probably the first luxury car Brad had seen in a while.

'Who's this woman anyway? A girlfriend?' Brad asked.

Brad was an old friend of the family and liked to keep himself acquainted with the lives of the townspeople.

'Nah, just a friend. Up in the Snowies for a holiday and clearly came off second best to a roo when she was driving last night.'

Brad raised an eyebrow. 'Well, your *friend* has a very expensive car. It won't be cheap to fix. Our other option is towing it out to Canberra. Either way it'll cost her.'

'Can you give me a quote to get it fixed here?'

Brad nodded and headed to the office at the front of the shop. He emerged a minute later with a slip of folded paper.

'That's with a ten percent discount, for your *friend*,' he said with a wink.

Liam shook Brad's hand and slipped the paper into the pocket of his jeans. 'Thanks, mate. Appreciate it.'

* * *

Pressing the doorbell at Gumtree Lakehouse left Liam's hand shaking. He didn't want Angie to think he was stalking her. He was only trying to help. But there had to be a reason she was in Gumtree Plains by herself. And without a car to get anywhere, it was going to be one long, boring holiday.

When the door opened, a sweet scent of freshly washed hair and perfume wafted into the open air. He'd never been a fan of sweet scents. On Angie though, it was what he imagined heaven might smell like.

'Liam, hi.'

'Hey, Angie. I have some news about your car.'

Her eyes grew wide and a smile spread across her face. 'Is it going to be okay?'

'I think you dodged a bullet on this one. I know a guy in town. Here.' He handed her the folded sheet of paper. 'This is a quote for the repair with a ten per cent discount. Said it'll take around two weeks.'

Angie's eyes glanced up and met his. 'Two weeks?' The disappointment in her voice was palpable.

'I'm sorry. Christmas is the worst time to have an accident.'

Angie opened the note and stared at it. She scrunched it up and stared at the ceiling, trying to hold back tears.

'This is the last thing I need with an impending—' she stopped herself before finishing the sentence. 'Christmas. An impending Christmas. The holidays are just so expensive these days.' She sniffled and wiped away the tears. 'I guess if I look at the bright side, at least I have insurance.'

The situation sucked and Liam's sinking heart plunged even further. Even when she was sad, she was beautiful. Effortless. Classic. No makeup to cover the light freckles on her face, or the tiny scar above her eyebrow. No concealer to hide the dark circles under her eyes. Angie was beautiful without even trying.

'I can lend you my car while you're here. I have the old ute and I don't mind driving it around. I'm home for the next two weeks.'

Angie shook her head. 'No way. The last thing I want to do is put you out more than I already have.'

'Put me out? You're not putting me out at all. It's what we do around here. Help our neighbours when they need it. Look, how about I head home and I'll be back in an hour with the other car.'

Angie shook her head. 'No, Liam. I couldn't possibly take your car —'

'It's too late,' Liam said as he headed back to the ute. 'You need transport out here. And if you want to repay me, I'll take a home cooked meal anytime in the next two weeks.'

He said a silent prayer as he headed out to the driveway, hoping this time she'd come through on calling him back.

CHAPTER SEVEN

Angie picked up her smartphone and dialled Lizzie's number. While she waited for Lizzie to pick up, she slid onto a slick metal stool at the breakfast bench and gazed out across the beautiful lake.

It was so still and calm under the overcast sky. The gum tree leaves hung low over the lake, providing adequate privacy for the house, and a distinct quietness Angie hadn't experienced on any other holiday.

The large glass windows and doors of the house enabled a full view of the lake. It was like being a queen perched on a pedestal amongst the Australian bushland.

'Hello?' The voice on the other end of the line was groggy.

'Lizzie, it's Ange.'

'You're alive. Why the hell didn't you call me when you got in? I was worried sick.'

'Worried sick? I don't have a missed call from you, so you can't have been too concerned,' Angie replied.

'Well, I *thought* about you. It's basically the same thing.'

Angie laughed. Sure, she could laugh about it now, but last night when she hit the kangaroo, she'd gotten the fright of her life. And now a massive repair bill to boot.

'How was the date?'

'Well,' Lizzie began. 'He was nice.'

'Nice?' Angie twirled a piece of blonde hair in her free hand and leaned into the marble stone bench. Since getting married, she couldn't get enough of Lizzie's failed dating stories and boozy hook-ups.

'So, you slept with him?'

'Actually no. We're going on a second date tomorrow night.'

'Wow, during the holidays? He must be super keen. Might as well get ready to meet his family and go shopping for a wedding dress.'

'Ah, more like super keen to get laid,' Lizzie responded. 'Couldn't keep his bloody hands to himself last night, which I didn't mind at all. He was hot. But probably just another fuck boy.'

'They're not all fuck boys, you know,' Angie said, not quite believing the comment herself.

'Tomato toh-mah-toh, I'll believe it when I see it,' Lizzie replied.

Angie rolled her eyes, but couldn't stop smiling. 'Have a little faith.'

'It's the truth. Anyway, is everything okay?' Lizzie asked.

Angie glanced around the large home, admiring the modern cream furniture and the spacious kitchen. The stainless-steel appliances almost sparkled above the white tiles and grey carpet.

When Angie looked back at the lake again, the smile disappeared. The truth was hard to swallow. It simply wasn't right to be sitting in front of such a breathtaking view and having no one to admire it with.

'Not really. I had an accident last night.'

'An accident? Are you alright?'

Angie sighed and swivelled on the stool. She was staring straight at the large fridge with French doors. The fridge that had no food in it because she had no transport to get groceries.

'I'm fine. I hit a kangaroo. And my car's in a shop. It needs to be repaired.'

'Are you hurt?'

The question made Angie touch her forehead. It still stung where she'd collided with the steering wheel.

'Not hurt. But you'll never guess who rescued me.'

'The Man from Snowy—'

'I'm serious, Lizzie.'

'Well don't keep me waiting.'

'It was Liam.'

A gasp sounded over the phone. 'Mr cunnilingus rescued you?'

I'm never going to live that down.

'Yes, Mr cunnilingus rescued me and brought me home. This morning he got a quote to get my car fixed and now he's off doing goodness knows what.'

'It's a trick.'

'What?'

'He wants you. Bad. He wanted you that day at the hut and he still wants you. And I think you should take him. For real this time. No third base bullshit. I'm talking all the way.'

Angie imagined Lizzie holding her thumb and index finger together in a circle while pumping her other index finger through the middle, like she always did when the topic of sex came up.

'Hmm, except for the fact I'm married, duh.'

'I don't care if you're a nun,' Lizzie replied. 'Your husband is a cheating scumbag who told you he's leaving you. You deserve to have some fun too.'

The comment didn't uplift Angie's mood. 'I'm still married. Michael might not give a shit about our vows, but I was serious when I said I'd stand by him through the good and bad times.'

'I have no words, Angie,' Lizzie said after a long sigh. 'Eli promised me he was a good guy. And now? I don't know what to believe.'

Elijah, Lizzie's closest male friend, worked in IT with Michael and vouched for him.

'Don't be silly. It's not your fault, or Eli's fault.' Angie was starting to wonder if any of them knew Michael at all.

'I guess in the end he showed his true colours. He's a cheating jerk,' Lizzie said.

The comment stung more than Angie was willing to admit. While Michael had treated her poorly, Angie had considered staying with him, *only* if she could trust he wouldn't do it again. It seemed impossible it would happen after what he'd said. Angie was a big believer in the saying, once a cheater, always a cheater. What did they have if they didn't have trust?

Still, the thought of staying faithful persisted. She'd taken a vow to remain faithful to him. She deserved better, but the constant nagging in the back of her mind convinced her if she left, she may never find anyone else.

The whole saga had left her stomach with the permanent sensation of falling from a sky-high building.

'I need to talk this out with him. Getting a divorce is a huge decision.'

'Oh, Angie. Would you cut it out? Michael's already made his decision. You fight for women's rights. You represent women in court whose husbands have cheated, abused them, abused their children and are trying to take everything from them. Their homes. Literally, the men in their lives are trying to take the clothes on their backs. It's now time to fight for yourself. If it's good enough for him—'

'Lizzie, I can't.' Angie pressed her fingers against her forehead. 'I can't keep reliving this nightmare of Michael leaving me a week before Christmas. I have to try and enjoy this holiday, because I can't come back to Canberra miserable and more exhausted than when I left.'

'Do you want me to come visit?'

'Of course I do, but you have family stuff. And Christmas is just around the corner. Look, I have to go. I'll call you later.'

'Before you go, there's something I have to tell you,' Lizzie revealed.

'What?'

'Someone tagged Michael in a photo on social media.'

'What do you mean someone tagged him in a photo? Who was it?'

'I don't know who it was. Some woman.'

'*Some woman*? Send me a screenshot.'

'No. I'm telling you out of respect so you'll stay off social media for now until this blows over.'

'Lizzie,' Angie demanded, 'Send me the damn photo.'

'No.'

'Elizabeth!'

A few seconds later, a message beeped on Angie's phone. When she saw it, she almost crumpled onto the floor.

It was a picture of a beautiful secluded beach in Hawaii. There was a tanned woman taking a photo of her toned legs as she lazed on the white sand.

In the distance was Michael's bare arse as he stared out over the light blue ocean. Angie would recognise that arse anywhere. Michael had gotten the red love heart tattooed on his bum cheek when he was eighteen and regretted it to this day.

Angie's lungs closed in as she gasped for air.

'Lizzie, I have to go.' When Angie ended the call, she clutched her hands to her chest and let the tears fall onto the marble bench. Her eyes stung with the betrayal of Michael's deceit. What was the point of all this? It seemed less likely than ever Michael would come home now. There was nothing left to salvage.

She stood up from the stool at the kitchen bench and headed downstairs to the master bedroom. The tiles were cold under her bare feet, making the reality of the situation even more stark.

It was almost a relief for the cold chill of the tiles to press into the soles of her feet, instead of being reminded of the constant aching in her heart.

When Angie reached the bottom of the stairs, the doorbell sounded.

'Bloody hell.' She turned on her heels and jogged back upstairs.

'Liam,' she said as she opened the door. 'What're you doing here?'

Despite her complete meltdown only moments before, it was impossible to ignore he looked even more delicious than the first day she'd met him on the brumby spotting tour.

Muscled legs filled bootleg jeans to the brim and his biceps flexed under a white t-shirt. She remembered the hardness of his muscles under the palms of her hands. The softness of his skin.

Angie hated to admit Liam was more attractive than her own husband.

In more ways than one.

'Hey there,' a woman's voice called out in the distance.

Angie looked over Liam's shoulder at the slim brunette waving at her next to Liam's ute. The skinny jeans emphasised her long legs and the tight polo shirt revealed a small baby bump.

Angie gulped.

'That's my sister-in-law, Jen.'

Angie's shoulders dropped as she released her breath. Why did she care if Liam was taken or not?

'Hello,' Angie said with a wave.

Liam wound a set of car keys around his index finger. 'I told you I'd come through for you. Now you can at least get around town and start enjoying your holiday.'

He stepped to the side. Sitting in the driveway was a white Mazda hatchback.

'I'll put a caveat on it and say it's not as nice as the Mercedes, but it'll get you from point A to point B.'

Angie stared at the car and then into Liam's grey eyes. Tears threatened to reveal themselves again.

His eyes resembled the colour of storm. They were the eyes of a man who was kind. His smile stretched across his face and his eyes crinkled in the corners. The image of him standing at the door of the holiday house, rescuing her once again, warmed her from the inside out.

Michael would never do something like this. Her own husband couldn't even show up to their Christmas holiday. Michael didn't even have the decency to break her heart in person. The ache in her heart forced more tears to emerge.

She couldn't help herself. Angie threw her arms around Liam's shoulders. As she hugged him and allowed the smell of his body to fill her nostrils, she sobbed into his t-shirt and cocooned herself in his warm embrace, wishing she'd never married Michael in the first place.

CHAPTER EIGHT

Her arms wrapped around his shoulders, making his skin tingle. It was the same sensation he'd experienced with her once before. A sensation he never wanted to end.

The touch of her bare skin against his in those short shorts and spaghetti strap shirt made his mind flash back to their heated encounter in the hut. The physical attraction for her was undeniable and it was difficult to fight the urge to run his hands slowly over her body again.

Instead, he lifted his arms and wrapped them around her waist, where his hands landed in the perfect curve of her back. The contact must've made her feel safe, because she nestled her face into his neck and tightened her grip around his shoulders.

Tears began to soak his shirt.

He hugged her tighter. Wanted to take her pain away. Know what was hurting her so deeply.

After a moment, Angie pulled away. She wiped the back of her hand under her nose.

'Gosh, I'm sorry. I've had a rough few days and I never expected anyone to show me such kindness. Where did you even come from?'

'Well, I came from Gumtree Plains, born and bred. And I'm showing you kindness because it's what we do for each other out here. It's what *friends* do for each other.'

The word *friends* caught in his throat. He longed for more than friendship with Angie, but the sparkling diamond ring on her left finger showed she had someone else. Permanently.

'Here are the keys,' he said as he handed over his beloved Mazda. 'Try not to hit another roo, okay?'

'I don't think I'll be driving in a storm at night for a while.'

Their fingers touched as Liam handed her the keys. When he looked up, their eyes met.

I'd give you my heart if you only asked for it.

She took the keys from him, ending their physical contact. Liam stepped away from Gumtree Lakehouse and headed back to his sister-in-law.

'Liam?' The sweet melody of Angie's voice forced him to hold his breath. He turned around, hoping she'd come through.

'You've been a wonderful friend to me. Let me return the favour. How about I make us dinner tonight. Jen's welcome too.'

Liam swallowed. Of course, there was no hidden meaning behind Angie's invitation. She was only trying to return the favour. Nothing would happen between them, not with that ring still in place. But Liam had never been one to turn down a free meal, and he did lend her his car.

'Count me in and let me know what time. You have my number—' Liam caught himself at the end of the sentence.

The same number she never called me on.

A shade of pink rose to Angie's cheeks as she smiled.

'Yes, I have your number. I'll text you once I've done some grocery shopping.'

'Guess I'll see you later tonight then.' Liam waved as he walked back to Jen and the ute. He pulled himself into the driver seat and put the key into the ignition.

'She seemed pretty relieved about this not being yours.' Jen stroked her pregnant belly.

'Pfft,' Liam replied as he put his left arm on the passenger head rest and began to reverse down the driveway. 'She's married. I have no chance.'

Jen pulled the seatbelt across her chest. 'Trust me. I'm a woman. I know those looks she was giving you. I don't care if she's married to a king. She likes you.'

Liam looked across at his sister-in-law. She was always trying to match-make him with her friends. None of the dates ever worked out because she was terrible at pairing personalities.

'No offence, Jen, but your track record with predicting future relationships hasn't been very successful.'

'I'm right this time. I bet.'

'Bet me what?' he asked as he powered the ute down the hill towards the main road. 'I bet you two will end up together. You can give me fifty bucks when it happens.'

'Is that all? Gee, you mustn't be very confident with your bet,' he teased.

'Fine. Two hundred bucks, I bet you two end up together. That's how confident I am, smart arse.'

Liam chuckled to himself. As much as he wanted it to be true, he couldn't believe it. Angie never called him after they'd shared an intimate afternoon together. She clearly moved on. And she was older than him, had an established career. Why would a woman like that give a simple country boy like him a second glance?

'When pigs fly, Jen. I'll be holding you to two hundred bucks when they do.'

***

He kept the phone close all day. Angie had promised to text him about dinner, but he wasn't sure she'd follow through.

Why didn't I just make a time?

As the hours ticked by, it seemed more likely it was a statement said in passing.

Liam threw the reins over the gate and began unsaddling the tall, muscular gelding.

After loosening the girth, he removed the saddle and placed it on the gate. The horse's back was covered in sweat after a midday workout down at the sand arena.

The horse snorted as Liam pulled the bridle off and replaced it with a halter. The bay gelding was Jen's horse, a dressage star, and the newest addition to the family at only six years old.

'How was he today?' Jen asked. She was standing by the paddock gate and stroked her hand down the gelding's brown face.

Despite being due in four months' time, the doctor suggested Jen give up riding for the remainder of her pregnancy. It was complicated. She'd had five miscarriages and severe morning sickness.

Harry, Liam's brother, and Jen had to be careful. This was the first pregnancy that'd come this far.

'Star was a *star* as usual. Did you expect anything less?'

Jen sighed as she rubbed her hands over her small baby bump. 'I wish I was up there in the saddle.' She turned her eyes to the gelding and rubbed her hands down his cheeks.

'I know this has been hard on you, but you'll be back in the saddle in no time. Probably with bubs on the back with you.'

'You betcha,' Jen replied, still running her hands down the gelding's face.

As Jen spoke the words, Liam's phone vibrated. He slid his hand in his pocket.

'Is it Angie?' Jen's face lit up as she asked the question.

Hope six o'clock isn't too early. I eat at the same time as my grandma ;)

Liam couldn't wipe the smile from his face as he slid the phone back into the pocket of his jeans.

Angie had followed through on her promise this time. Of course, he knew he didn't have a chance in hell with her, but he wasn't about to turn down dinner with a beautiful woman.

'Bloody hell, Liam, don't keep it a secret!' Jen said, almost jumping up and down on the gravel driveway.

'Dinner at six o'clock tonight.'

Jen pumped her fist into the air and did a little dance, kicking the rocks and gravel in all directions under her riding boots.

'Calm down, would you? It's not a date. It's only dinner with an old friend.'

'An old friend? Please, you totally like her. And I can't wait to tell everyone when you guys get together it was my doing.'

Jen was like a big sister to him and had been through so much already. He figured it wouldn't hurt to let her have her pride this one time.

'I'm going to text Angie back. In the meantime, I'd better take a shower.' He lifted his arm and smelled his pit.

'Yikes. I'll never get asked back again if I go there smelling like this.'

CHAPTER NINE

Why?

It was the question Angie kept asking herself as she rushed around the kitchen, wiping down the benches and placing a pie into the oven.

Why did I invite him over for dinner?

Liam was Angie's kryptonite. She'd never had a one-night stand until she met Liam.

It's not like it was really a one-night stand. We didn't go all the way.

But it was far enough for her to have developed a connection with him. It was why she never slept with guys she'd just met. Angie had thought about Liam almost every second of the day after their rendezvous in the hut.

She used to wake up from dreams, sweating from the memory of his rough hands running over her smooth skin, between her legs and over her breasts. She'd glance down and notice pert nipples under her nightgown. So many times, she'd come close to calling him. And then she didn't.

What would come of their relationship? He was three years her junior. A cowboy. Their lives were worlds apart. She didn't think she was better than him, but worried if she got in too deep, she wouldn't be able to pull herself away. Another broken heart wasn't something she wanted to rush into.

Sure, the endorphins of a new love left her feeling on top of the world, but in her experience, it was always followed by heartache.

Yet despite her reservations, no one had left Angie as satisfied as Liam did back on that April afternoon. Now she was getting to know him, the regret of never calling him tugged at her heart. Made her realise what a fool she'd been.

But could they really have had a chance? Maybe. If she'd taken a chance on him she might not be in the position she was in now.

Michael's betrayal had played on her mind all day. More than anything, she dreaded having the title of divorcee next to her name. Marriage was sacred and something shared between two people who loved each other unconditionally. It was a promise to be with the other person until the very end. Apparently not for Michael. What made her think she was any different to the two wives that came before her?

How could I have been so bloody stupid?

Angie glanced at the clock.

Shit.

She had ten minutes to get showered and changed. Taking two steps at a time, she fled downstairs to the shower.

After the shower, she stood in the bedroom in a towel as she pulled out a long, flowing black and white Aztec maxi dress. The outfit always showed off a bit of cleavage and hugged her hips. It seemed a bit too revealing for a dinner with someone who was supposed to only be a friend.

Friend.

Lizzie told her to have sex with Liam, but it seemed wrong. Angie could never cheat because she'd been cheated on. The devastation and utter heartbreak had almost killed her the first time around. But a part of her questioned why Michael got to have a summer fling while she was left behind.

Maybe Lizzie was right. The way Michael had treated her was unacceptable, and waiting for him to come home was useless. After seeing the photo of Michael on the beach with *that* woman, butt-naked and totally carefree, Angie was certain of one thing. Michael wasn't coming back.

She stared at the maxi dress laid out on the bed. After dropping the towel on the bedroom floor, she held up the dress and stepped into it. The satin material flowed down her legs as she pulled it towards her neck.

It was almost cathartic.

Once it was on, she let the fabric fall glide across her feet. She ran her hands down the silky material, and over her breasts, her tummy and her hips, imagining they weren't her hands, but Liam's hands.

The doorbell rang and sounded through the entire house, jolting her back to the present moment.

She jogged up the stairs with damp hair, and when she opened the door, Liam stood tall on the other side. He was the picture of her perfect man. A real cowboy. It was as if those jeans had been fitted by a tailor. His muscles popped and filled them to the brim. The black v-line shirt showed off the beginning of his chest hair. When he saw her, his gaze quickly ran over her body.

When his eyes finally met hers, he smiled, and the dimples in the corners of his mouth melted her heart. Angie held her ground, finding stability by holding onto the door.

'I thought you might like some flowers to brighten up the house. It's a bit beige if you ask me,' he said as he pulled a fresh bouquet from behind his back.

Angie gasped. 'Sunflowers. They're beautiful.' Plucking up the courage, she stepped close and kissed his freshly-shaved cheek. Cologne wafted into her nostrils, almost bringing her undone.

When she stepped back, she admired the flowers once again. The stark yellow petals would certainly brighten up the house and liven up what'd been a very dark holiday so far.

'Thank you so much,' Angie said, losing herself in Liam's eyes.

'Is something burning?' Liam asked, looking over her shoulder into the kitchen.

Angie was still daydreaming. 'What?'

'There's smoke coming from the kitchen.'

'Oh no.' Angie's stomach tightened into a knot. When she turned around, the kitchen was filled with smoke. Then the fire alarm started to whir.

'Shit!' She ran into the kitchen, heading straight for the oven. On opening the door, she stepped back and coughed as smoke filled her lungs. As she turned around, she tripped over her own feet. She expected to land flat on her face on the tiles.

Instead, Liam reached his hands under her arms, catching and lifting her to her feet. She swung around to face him.

Despite the smoky kitchen, she couldn't forget the cologne that ignited her senses only moments before.

Her hands lay on his muscled chest and she stared up into his blue eyes as he held her a little too close. The eyes of the man, who brought her so much pleasure in an outback hut in the middle of the Snowy Mountains, was melting her heart all over again.

This was dangerous.

He was dangerous.

'I'll take care of the alarm.' Liam's hands fell away from her body, so he could grab a tea towel and wave it under the fire alarm.

Angie had to catch her breath. The whirring perforated in her ears and she pressed her hands over them to try and drown out the sound.

The fire alarm switched off after a moment. The house was peaceful again.

Liam headed over to the glass windows in front of the balcony. He unclipped them from the floor and pulled them across, revealing a wooden balcony overlooking the lake. Now, it was at a private open-air restaurant.

'Wow, I didn't know you could open those doors onto the balcony,' Angie said.

Liam turned back and smiled as he ran his hand across his forehead, wiping away the perspiration.

'Couldn't let you leave without seeing this view.'

Angie stared at Liam from the kitchen. She imagined how foolish she must've looked drooling over him like a lust-filled teenage girl. Blood pumped quickly through her veins. She was a food-deprived lioness, watching Liam like he was her next meal.

'Did you want to check on what's in the oven?'

'Oh, of course.' Angie jumped at his suggestion, thankful he'd broken the silence and pulled her thoughts away from what she wanted to do to him. She kneeled down and looked at the black pie she was planning to serve for dinner.

'Well, we won't be having pie,' she announced. It was difficult to hide the disappointment in her voice. It'd taken her all afternoon to prepare that meal.

'What else do you have in the fridge?' Liam asked. 'I'm sure we can find something to eat.'

Angie stood and wiped her hands down the satin maxi dress. This wasn't how she wanted dinner to pan out. The image she had in her mind was one where she swanned around the house, wearing a maxi dress and commanded attention like a goddess, followed by some pie, dessert and maybe a goodnight kiss.

'There's not much in there,' she admitted, a little defeated.

Liam headed into the kitchen and opened the fridge. 'Let's see what you have in the fridge. I'm sure we can whip something up.'

CHAPTER TEN

Liam wasn't much of a cook, yet he'd be lying if he said he didn't know *anything*. Mum loved to cook and he had inherited some of her skills. One of those was pulling together meals on the small amount of food left in the fridge at the end of the week.

When Liam was at university, he never wasted a vegetable, and always pulled off a batch of soup with something. This would be a piece of cake.

As he noted the items in the fridge and started making a mental list of what they might be able to create. It was a good distraction from drooling over Angie in a figure-hugging maxi dress mere inches away.

Jesus, she was a showstopper. The material hugged her figure in all the right places and her cleavage was...

Stop it.

He didn't want to get hard in the kitchen.

If only he could kiss her again. If only she wasn't wearing that damned wedding ring. Being the other man wasn't the person he wanted to become.

Still, Angie was unlike anyone he'd ever met before. Her cute smile and cropped blonde hair had his heart stopping each time he laid eyes on her.

'Anything we can use to muster a meal?'

Angie's voice pulled Liam from his internal dilemma. He quickly began grabbing things out.

'I think we'll be able to make something. More of a light meal though. I hope you like cheese and olives.'

After a few minutes, they had a pretty acceptable platter for two. Liam was pretty impressed with his effort.

'Liam, you saved the day. Well, the night.' She looked up at him from behind her short blonde hair.

It took all his strength to not reach down and push the hair behind her ears. To lean down and kiss those soft, pink lips. Lips he'd kissed before. Lips he'd kill to kiss again.

'How about we take this onto the balcony. I'll bring the platter and you bring the plates,' he said, trying to take his mind off Angie.

She leaned down into the cupboard and pulled out two plates and two wine glasses.

'Want a glass of wine?' Angie pulled a bottle of white wine from the fridge and tipped it towards him.

Now the night was starting. 'I'd love one.'

Angie walked onto the balcony where she put the plates and wine glasses on the table. The dress flowed in the mild wind, exposing her bare feet.

Christ she was beautiful. The vision of her reminded him of the free-spiritedness of a wild brumby.

Liam could imagine it now. Living with Angie would be easy. It all seemed so natural being with her in this house.

He placed the platter in the middle of the table, before leaning over and pulling out the chair for Angie to sit down.

'Such a gentleman. I can't remember the last time someone did that for me.'

Wow, not even her own husband?

Liam took his own seat. 'I only do it when I'm on holidays. You know, special occasions.'

'This is a special occasion?'

Shit.

Any time spent with Angie was special, though he couldn't exactly admit that.

'Two friends who haven't seen each other in a long time. I argue it's a special occasion.'

'*Friends*. Is that what we are?'

'I guess so,' he replied, not knowing how to label their relationship.

Angie smiled and grabbed a few olives, crackers and dip for her plate.As they picked food off the platter and sipped from their wine, one question remained on the tip of his tongue.

No.

It burned.

His better judgment told him he shouldn't venture there tonight. Why ruin a perfectly good night with insecure questions about the past? As much as he tried to fight it, he couldn't sit there playing friends and not at least ask why.

'You look like you want to say something,' Angie said as she picked up an olive and popped it into her mouth.

A light breeze picked up and brushed over the lake, leaving a soft ruffle on the surface of the water. The gum trees swayed slowly in the breeze.

It was like having their own private paradise.

'Why didn't you call me?' The question had been playing on his mind for the past eight months.

Angie wiped the corners of her mouth with a napkin, then rested her hands on the table. 'The honest truth is, I didn't know if it'd work out between you and I. You're younger and I questioned whether we were on the same maturity level as me.'

Ouch.

Liam had always been mature for his age. He'd even dated older women in the past. Angie though, was a different woman altogether.

'Of course, I've seen differently these last few days. You've been amazing.'

A smile threatened to break. 'Thanks, I guess.'

'It's nothing against you, Liam. In fact, that afternoon in the hut was the most passionate, crazy, intimate thing I've ever done with anyone. I've never had a one-night stand before. I've always been in long-term relationships. You're something else entirely to anyone I've ever met. Maybe, in a way, I didn't want to ruin it in case we didn't work out.'

Liam appreciated her honesty. All her points were valid, but she still hadn't given them a shot. By denying them the opportunity, did it mean they'd never have a chance to see if they were *meant* to be together?

Maybe Angie was the woman Liam was supposed to be with. Now he'd never know.

'Does *that* have something to do with it?' Liam glanced at her left hand where the diamond encrusted ring sat snug around her dainty finger.

Angie sighed. '*This* was a mistake,' she said as she held up her finger and examined the ring. 'I've been married two months, with the guy for five, and it's all fallen apart.'

Her gaze moved towards the lake.

'Actually, it isn't falling apart. It's already shattered into a million pieces.'

He didn't know what to say. 'I'm sorry to hear that.'

Angie's shoulders slumped.

'This could be the wine talking, but I'm going to say it anyway. I should've called you, Liam. If I could go back in time, I would. Maybe things would be different. Who knows, maybe I'd be married to *you* instead.'

Angie giggled as she sipped from the glass of white wine.

It was almost as if he wasn't there at all and she'd muttered the thought out loud to herself.

Liam watched as she looked out into the distance. Then he spotted a rogue tear stream down her pale cheek.

Hearing Angie say those words made his heart ache. Her brave face stayed composed as she sipped the wine.

Liam didn't want to be the jerk who sat back and watched her cry. So, he stood up and walked over to her chair.

He knelt on the balcony, took her hands in his, and stared into her glowing hazel eyes.

As she cried, his heart constricted. Without thinking, he stood to his feet and pulled her up with him.

When she was standing, he lifted her arms over his shoulders and wrapped his arms around her waist. Angie took one last breath before nestling her head into his chest.

Without saying a word, their bodies flowed to the rhythm of the wind and they slow- danced to imaginary music, barefoot on the timber balcony, overlooking the lake as the sun set and descended them into darkness.

CHAPTER ELEVEN

There was no coming back from this. None. Was this what it was like to be appreciated? Wanted?

Of course, Michael gave her all those things at the start, but not like this. To be held. Cherished. Guarded like she was the most precious woman on earth.

She still remembered the way Liam left her skin tingling that day. The breathlessness in her lungs. The sheer exhaustion that overtook her body.

Now, they were slow-dancing on the balcony at a holiday house in Gumtree Plains. The very place where they first met.

A mere eight months later, Angie was in the same place with the same man, yet she was married to someone else.

It seemed strange now, like her real life was a movie she could only replay in her mind. There was no touching it or reliving it, only the memories that cycled through her mind.

In this moment, her reality didn't seem tangible. Being in Liam's arms made her realise she'd made a terrible mistake. She should've taken a chance and called him.

One thing she didn't admit to him when he asked why she never called, was she cared what people would think. Michael was everything she wanted in a husband. Successful, wealthy and well-respected. Having him on her arm was something to be proud of. But Angie knew now that the appearance of a nice life didn't mean she was living one.

Liam was nothing like the other guys she'd dated. It was in fact Michael who was the same as all her past boyfriends. Selfish. Destructive. Liam was the exception. The problem was this time she'd married one of *them*. The wrong man.

Liam's hands stayed in the curve of her back, embracing her in his strong grip. She never wanted to leave this place. The lake house. His arms. Her cheek nuzzled into his warm chest. His beating heart thudded against her ear.

It was strange how Liam's warm body gave her a sense of safety like nothing else. Michael had given her financial stability, but never this kind of serenity. The cocoon Liam surrounded her with calmed her senses and gave her the strength to believe she would get through everything life had thrown at her the past few days.

Maybe coming on this holiday was meant to happen.

Fate.

Perhaps Lizzie was right. Perhaps Angie should explore what might be with Liam.

Michael hadn't bothered to make contact after he told her he wanted a divorce. She pictured it in her mind as she slow-danced with Liam. The long nights of booze and cigars near a bonfire on the beach, making love to a beautiful, tanned model who was probably barely in her twenties. The life with no responsibilities to anyone was the life Michael was used to leading. Carefree and only ever worrying about himself and his own needs.

But what about Angie's needs?

She lifted her head off Liam's chest and looked up into his grey eyes. Somehow, they seemed brighter under the setting sun.

Her feet stopped moving.

'Are you okay?' he asked.

'I haven't been this okay in a while,' she replied. Slowly, she moved her hands over his shoulders and onto his chest. The muscles tensed under her palms. Her hands quivered. Liam's hands didn't move from the curve of her back. Instead, he stared down at her, his gaze fixed on her eyes.

'Would it be okay if I kissed you?' she asked.

Liam's gaze didn't change. 'Are you sure you want to do that?'

So much had happened, it was almost moving too fast for her to keep up. This was all out of her comfort zone. Going on a holiday alone. Finding out her cheating husband wasn't coming home for Christmas because he'd met someone else. That he was already initiating a separation.

The only thing she knew for sure was she wanted to kiss Liam right here, right now. To be held in his arms, enveloped in his love.

She stood on her tippy toes so their lips were almost touching. His breath brushed over her face and she closed her eyes, wishing things were different.

Carefully, she pressed her lips into his. Liam's hands tightened around her waist and she gripped her arms around his shoulders.

And like magic, under the stars on a balcony overlooking Gumtree Lake, Angie kissed the man that haunted her dreams.

* * *

It was mid-morning when Liam placed one final kiss on Angie's lips before heading out the front door.

His sexy hips swayed as he jogged to the ute in bare feet and climbed into the driver's seat.

Heat rose from her chest and into her cheeks as she waved goodbye. The previous night was a dream she didn't want to wake up from.

They didn't have sex. Liam was adamant.

At first, Angie wasn't happy. Why did she have to hold out while Michael fucked whoever he wanted?

When she thought about what Liam was saying, she was glad he abstained.

Not one to rush things.

Angie closed the front door of the house and headed downstairs to the shower. Half an hour later, she emerged fresh and ready for the day.

The phone buzzed on the bed. It was Liam's number. Angie's body tingled as she answered the phone.

'Hello, handsome. Missing me already?'

'Angie, it's Jen. Liam's sister-in-law.'

Angie swallowed.

That's embarrassing.

The last thing she wanted was for Jen to get the wrong idea about her intentions with Liam.

'Hi, Jen. What can I do for you?'

'I hope you don't mind. Liam's phone was sitting on the bench and

I couldn't resist calling. Listen, we're having Christmas lunch tomorrow and I'd love if you came.'

Liam had mentioned Christmas lunch with his family. In typical Angie style, she didn't want to impose and politely declined. Liam had offered Christmas dinner instead at the holiday house, just the two of them. It seemed romantic. And much better than being forced to sit through another family gathering with people she didn't know.

'That's a lovely offer,' Angie replied. 'But I don't want to intrude, so I'll have to decline.'

'Here's the thing,' Jen began. 'Liam is super shy about it, but Christmas day is actually his birthday.'

What?

Why hadn't he told her? He'd purposely omitted that bit of information when he'd mentioned Christmas lunch with his family.

'He's not big on gifts and hates people making a fuss, so I thought this would be the perfect birthday surprise. You know, given you guys are *old* friends.'

Old friends.

It was ridiculous given the circumstances. Angie considered it for a moment. Maybe it would be a nice surprise. Besides, sitting in a holiday house all alone on Christmas Day wasn't something too appealing.

'Okay, Jen. Sounds like a great idea. I'd love to come.'

'Brilliant!' Jen exclaimed into the phone. 'This is going to be the best birthday present ever. See you tomorrow at ten a.m.'

CHAPTER TWELVE

Liam woke to the smell of sizzling bacon and eggs wafting from the kitchen. There was no doubt about Mum. She loved to cook.

Rolling onto his back, he stretched his arms wide and let out a long yawn. It also happened to be his birthday, and he figured she was up to no good. Mum always gave him a special side of something for his birthday at breakfast. Family tradition.

When Liam threw the doona off his legs, he cast a thought to Angie, alone at Gumtree Lakehouse. Sure, she had a quaint balcony overlooking the lake to sit on during breakfast while she sipped a hot cup of coffee, but she was all alone on Christmas day. He wished he could slip away without a word to his family, so he could spend the day with her.

At least I'll be seeing her tonight.

A quick glance at the alarm clock showed it was only nine thirty. Counting down the hours would be like staring at a wall. All he had to do was make it through the day and then he could disappear.

In the kitchen, the smells of home cooking ignited a grumble in his stomach.

'There's my birthday boy,' Mum said when she turned and spotted Liam.

The apron tied around her waist was decorated in Christmas trees and tinsel. The Christmas carols were already cranked up in the living room on the ancient stereo system, and Grandad was swaying around the room with his mug of coffee, singing the lyrics to Jingle Bells.

'Dad!' Liam's father yelled across the dining table from behind the newspaper. 'If you spill coffee on the carpet, you'll be cleaning it up,' he growled. 'We never did get out that stain of red wine from last year.'

Grandad stopped dancing long enough to stare at his son. 'It's Christmas. Don't be the Grinch,' he retorted.

Liam laughed. Grandad certainly still had some wits about him.

'Sit down, sweetie, and I'll grab your breakfast.' Mum went back into the kitchen and plated up Liam's birthday breakfast.

He sat down next to Dad who peered at him over the newspaper. The entrenched lines in his forehead were a little less deep today. The old man deserved a day off. He worked hard enough year-round. Liam only wished he'd take better care of himself and rest when he needed it.

'Happy birthday, Son.'

'Thanks, Watson.'

Dad's eyes crinkled in the corners. Liam loved getting a rise out of him.

'You know I love you, Dad.'

Watson smiled and continued reading the newspaper. Mum walked back to the dining table and put down a full plate of bacon, eggs, sausages and baked beans. Then she put down a bowl with a tea towel over the top.

'Mum's Christmas and birthday surprise. Voila,' she said as she lifted the tea towel and revealed a steaming bowl of pudding with Brandy cream drizzled over the top. 'Fresh out of the oven, so it's still warm.'

Liam's stomach purred. 'Thanks, Mum.'

Mum leaned down and kissed Liam on the forehead. 'Only the best for my boy.'

Liam dipped a fork into the pudding, twisted it in the dollop of cream and lifted it to his mouth. As it melted, he closed his eyes and savoured the sweet hot ingredients on his tongue.

Brandy cream. Mum knows me too well.

He was about to take another bite, when Jen walked through the sliding door carrying bags of food and presents, followed by Harry, Liam's older brother.

'Happy Birthday,' Jen said as she dropped the bags in the kitchen and headed to the dining table to give Liam a kiss.

'I'll take whatever he's having,' Harry said as he kissed Mum on the cheek.

'Sorry, only for the birthday boy.'

Harry stared at Mum and asked, 'Why does he get pudding and Brandy cream for breakfast?'

'Because it's my birthday,' Liam replied with a grin.

'So?' Harry asked as he glared at Liam.

Liam stabbed another piece of pudding on the fork and pointed it at Harry. 'When you have to share your birthday with the birth of Jesus Christ and pretty much everyone else on the planet, then you can have some pudding and Brandy cream for breakfast. Until then, let me eat my pudding in peace.' Liam twirled the pudding in the Brandy cream and took a bite.

'You spoil him, Mum,' Harry muttered as he started packing food into the fridge.

'And I have a surprise,' Jen said to Liam as she rubbed her hands together like an evil mastermind up to no good.

'Is it more food? Because the way to my heart is through my stomach.'

'I guess it's a good thing I brought cookies then.'

Liam was still looking at Jen, but the words didn't come from her mouth.

The house fell silent. Liam glanced at the front door where everyone else was looking.

Angie stood there like an angel. The sunlight hit her hair at all the right angles, making her glow. The aqua and white floral dress fell to the ground, revealing petite cream sandals and pink painted toes. Her hair was straight and pinned back on one side, showing off her soft, pale skin.

Liam swallowed and dropped his fork on the table.

'Angie, what're you doing here?'

The room stayed quiet.

'A little birdie told me it's your birthday today. And I can't say no to a good party.' She stepped into the house holding the container of baked goods. 'I promise this time I haven't burnt the food. There won't be any fire alarms today.'

Jen's hand rested on Liam's shoulder.

He looked up at her, and she winked back.

'You're unbelievable,' he whispered as he got to his feet.

'Just doing the good work of Cupid,' she whispered back.

When Liam reached Angie, he grabbed her hands and leaned in to kiss her on the cheek.

'This is a surprise,' he whispered.

'A good one, I hope.'

'Are you kidding? It's the best birthday present ever.'

* * *

'So, Angie. What brings you to Gumtree Plains for the holidays?'

Liam knew Mum would be interested in Angie's life. He'd only ever brought one girl home before, so it was somewhat of a novelty. And Angie was a successful lawyer, so Mum wanted to know everything, including Angie's intentions with her son. But the serious line of questioning was impacting the mood of the day.

'I was supposed to come here with someone. When they couldn't attend, I decided to come alone. I'd already paid for the booking at Gumtree Lakehouse and needed a holiday.'

'Who were you coming with?'

Angie cleared her throat and her eyes shifted to Liam.

Shit.

If he'd known Angie was coming over, he could've prepped his family and let them know the situation. Let the news settle in before she arrived. Now they were going to think he was having an affair with a married woman.

Grounds for a lecture and a severe talking to.

'My husband,' Angie replied. 'Well, my *estranged* husband.'

Still looking ridiculous in the Christmas apron, Mum shot a blunt stare at Liam across the table.

The second woman he'd brought home was married. Mum's lecture later on was going to be one to remember.

'It's complicated,' Angie continued. 'My husband is, well, we're no longer together and getting a divorce. So we're separated. Hence the estranged part.'

There was a collective raising of eyebrows at the table. This was information Angie omitted to reveal to Liam last night.

'I'm sorry to hear that,' Mum replied as she poured herself a glass of wine. 'Liam went through a similar thing recently. His high school sweetheart married his best friend last week. It was after Damo and

Bec, you know, got together while Liam and Bec were still—'

Liam shot out of his seat with the bowl of potatoes. 'Baked potato, anyone?'

It seemed they both had secrets they didn't want to air to the world.

'Please,' Angie said, lifting her plate.

As he popped a couple of crispy potatoes onto the plate, he looked down and spotted her strained smile.

CHAPTER THIRTEEN

Angie dropped her handbag on the carpet and slumped into the couch after slamming the front door of Gumtree Lakehouse shut. It was exactly why she didn't want to go to Liam's family home for Christmas lunch.

They were nice enough, except his mum's interrogation. The woman was throwing bombs from all directions and Angie was expected to dodge them all or she'd fall down.

After eating all the calorie-laden food on offer, the thought of dinner made her stomach churn. Despite the food and awkward conversation, it was wonderful to see Liam in his natural surroundings. He was so relaxed and calm around his family. There was a distinct quietness about him she hadn't seen before. And the way he looked at her when she arrived on his birthday was priceless. If she could relive that moment over again, she would.

After taking a moment to catch her breath, she pushed herself off the couch and waddled to the kitchen. With a sizeable belly after lunch, she was sure people might suspect she was carrying a little more than some extra Christmas pudding.

She flicked the switch on the kettle and steam began to rise from the spout. The view of the lake from kitchen ran as far as the eye could see. Yet even the beauty of Gumtree Plains couldn't stop her mind from running to what Liam's mum said. His high school sweet-heart had broken his heart and married another man.

His best friend to be precise.

How selfish she'd been to not suspect Liam was going through something too. She was foolish to think she was the only person who'd ever been hurt in a relationship.

The kettle popped and brought her attention back to the boiled water. She pulled a peppermint teabag from the cupboard, along with a mug, and filled it to the brim.

Peppermint tea always calmed her belly. In and out, she dropped the tea bag into the water. Finally, when the tea was dark enough, she put the teabag in the bin and headed to the couch. As she sat down, the tin roof began to tick tack with the pitter patter of rain.

Angie looked over her shoulder to the balcony and noticed grey clouds moving quickly over Gumtree Plains.

The Snowy Mountains was so beautiful. Sometimes hauntingly so. Even though she loved her job as a lawyer, leaving this place would be hard.

* * *

The sound of the doorbell woke Angie up from a sleep. Her eyes opened and shut as they adjusted to the darkness of the house. The rain was now pelting down on the metal roof. A rumble of thunder struck, and she jolted at the sound.

The doorbell rang again. At least after a nap her stomach wasn't so heavy with rich Christmas lunch.

She pushed herself off the white leather couch and headed to the door. When she opened it, Liam was standing outside in a saturated white t-shirt. The wet shirt clung to his body, revealing everything Angie had wanted to see and touch ever since they'd first met. His hair dripped from the ends, and he shivered in the cool air.

'Liam, get inside.' Angie grabbed his hand and ushered him into the house.

His hair dripped onto the carpet as he rubbed his hands up and down his arms. Angie slammed the door shut behind him.

'Shit, it's cold out there for a summer day. Haven't seen this much rain in years.'

Angie ran downstairs to the laundry to grab a few towels.

Upstairs, Liam peeled his shirt off. Angie watched on in silence. It was like their first encounter replaying itself all over again.

She headed for the couch and handed him the towel. 'What were you doing out in the rain?'

'I must've pressed the doorbell five times before you answered.

The rain was coming from all angles out there. That's why I'm soaked.'

Angie sat on the couch, crossed her legs and watched as Liam wiped the towel down his arms and chest. She was trying to look cool and calm, but couldn't ignore the trembling between her legs.

'I may have been having an afternoon siesta.'

'More like a refresh from my Mum's persistent questions. I'm sorry about today. She's not normally like that.'

Angie waved her hand in the air. 'Don't stress about it. It's fine. I've had way worse in a court room.'

Liam stared at her from across the living room. 'Well, if it makes you feel any better, you showing up was a great surprise. In fact, it was the best birthday present I've ever received. And I love you met my family.'

Love.

There was that four-letter word. Liam didn't seem to have any problems expressing himself. It was nice knowing where she stood.

Angie folded her arms across her chest and tried to think of something unsexy, because the sight of Liam was raising the temperature in the room.

'I'm happy I met them too.'

In all honesty, she never felt like she belonged with Michael's family the way she did with Liam's. Especially Jen. Liam's sister-in-law was a beautiful woman.

Liam sat on the couch next to her. 'I'm happy you're happy.' He put his hand on hers, clearly not realising what that did to her. She'd had Liam once. But once wasn't enough.

It was cruel. Like only eating one square of chocolate when she wanted the entire block. Liam was like an addiction she couldn't kick. The flashbacks of his hands on hers, skin touching skin, was etched in her memory, haunting her in the depths of the night.

'I'm sorry about what happened with your...ex,' Angie said as she squeezed his hand.

Liam shrugged and leaned back into the couch. 'What's done is done. Besides, I've moved on.'

His eyes traced her body up and down as he squeezed her hand in return.

The sight brought back the memory of the photo Lizzie had sent her. Michael. The beach. The sexy model. His naked body. She wasn't to blame for the end of their marriage. Michael was the one who cheated. He was the one who left her at the airport and broke the news over the phone. The coward couldn't even face her before he began an affair. Angie had stayed faithful, true to Michael, like she had to the all the boyfriends before.

Lizzie was right. Now was Angie's time.

Angie grabbed Liam's hand and squeezed it as tight as she could. 'I've moved on as well.' She leaned over the couch and allowed her lips to kiss his once again.

Liam sat up and pressed his lips into hers. Peppermint. And the sweet scent of aftershave. The smells overloaded her senses, bringing her body to life.

'I know you said we should wait, but I don't want to.'

Liam pulled away. 'Angie, you're still married. That complicates things.'

'My marriage is over. My husband left me for another woman. It's done.'

Liam sat back on the couch and ran his hand through his damp hair. 'Angie, I don't want to be your rebound.'

Ouch.

Angie licked her lips where the taste of peppermint lingered. She sat back into the couch next to him.

How could she respond? She didn't think of Liam as the rebound, but understood why he might feel like one. 'It's not like that at all.' She looked across at him and caught his eyes.

They'd never know whether their relationship would last the distance if they didn't at least try.

'I want this. I want you. All of you. And not for a night. I want to see where this could go, you and I, and if there's a chance we could share a future together.'

She leaned in once more and their lips touched. Trying to resist was useless. Angie yearned for Liam's touch. To succumb to him. To again experience the breathlessness and contentment that overcame her body when she was in Liam's arms.

The kiss became deeper, more passionate and Liam pressed his hands into the side of Angie's cheeks, holding her close to him. Angie pushed him back into the couch.

Lifting one leg, she pulled her dress up over her thighs, straddling him, and lowered herself onto his lap. He pulled her close and began kissing her collarbone.

Angie arched her back as Liam ran his hands under her dress, following the curves of her body. It left her skin tingling, yearning for more.

'Liam,' she breathed. 'I'm scared.'

'It's okay,' he replied, not letting his lips leave her skin. 'We don't have to do anything you don't want to.'

'I want you. I've wanted you ever since my birthday at the hut, and I don't want to wait any longer.'

Her hands fell to his cheeks, allowing the sharp stubble to run across the palms of her hands. 'I think we should take this to the bedroom.'

'Are you sure?' Liam's grey eyes shone under the lights of the house.

'I've never been more certain.' Angie slid off Liam's lap and took his hand, leading him downstairs to the bedroom.

They stood at the end of the bed. She grabbed the hem of Liam's shirt and slowly lifted it up over his head. Under his shirt was a sculpted body, tanned from working out in the sun. It was exactly how she remembered it. The belt buckle shone under the bedroom light. Her hands reached for it, un-clicking it and letting it fall open.

In return, Liam slipped Angie's dress off her shoulders, exposing her collarbone. The dress slid over her arms and fell to the floor.

'You're so beautiful,' Liam whispered as he traced the line of her cleavage with his index finger.

Angie unclipped the back of her bra and let it fall to the floor, exposing her breasts. With each piece of clothing she removed, it was like removing the baggage she'd been carrying on her shoulders when Michael told her he was leaving for good. She was letting go of Michael and her marriage, ready to move on. Ready for the man she was supposed to be with.

Liam unzipped his pants and pulled off his jeans. They were both standing in their underwear. Almost naked.

Liam stepped forward, taking her hands in his. He intertwined his fingers in hers, tangling them in a complicated web. Angie pulled his hands toward her, forcing them into the curve of her back. Her breasts pressed against his chest and she looked up at him.

So much mystery was yet to be uncovered.

His eyes gazed down into hers, taking in the sight of her naked body. Spinning her in a circle, Liam lay Angie onto the bed. Gently using his knee, he parted her legs and lowered the weight of his body onto hers. It was more than she was expecting. Nonetheless, the heaviness of his body on hers brought her a sense of safety.

'Hold on,' she said, remembering the condoms she'd bought at the shop a few days ago.

'That's rather presumptuous of you. I'm not the kind of guy to sleep around, you know,' Liam joked as he lowered his lips to her mouth.

'I'm hoping you'll let your guard down, just this once,' Angie teased as she handed the wrapper to him.

Liam smiled and sat back on his knees. After he pulled off his briefs, he slipped on the protection.

He then tucked his fingers between her hips and the fabric of her panties, slid them down her legs and threw them off the bed. He parted her legs and began to kiss the inside of her thighs.

Angie arched her back and moaned, unable to stop the flood rushing through the core of her body to the place Liam's lips were touching.

Her skin tingled under Liam's touch, sending each and every nerve ending into overdrive.

'Liam.' A moan escaped her lips without warning. It was more intense this time. Now that she'd gotten to know him, she was starting to fall for him. His charm. The kindness in his heart.

Liam lifted his head and stared at her from between her legs.

'I want you now, Liam.' She wrapped her hands around his forearms and pulled him up, so his body weighed upon hers. 'You have no idea how long I've wanted this.' Her hands travelled down his muscled back to his behind. She wrapped her fingers around him and pulled him inside her.

At first, she thought she might be out of practice. But her legs instinctively wrapped around his body, interlocking at her ankles, and she held him closer than she'd ever held anyone before.

Their bodies moved together like one, their rhythm matching perfectly. His lips moved between her collarbone and her lips, never leaving her skin.

Every nerve ending and fibre in her body lit up like a firework. As the motions became faster and more intense, Angie's legs wrapped tighter around Liam's body, and she clasped her fingers into his skin as they made love into the night.

* * *

Liam's index finger drew patterns across the skin on her back, leaving a trail of tingling skin. She was lying on her stomach in bed while Liam lay on his side staring at her.

'Why are you looking at me like that?'

'Because you're beautiful,' he said, still drawing patterns with his finger.

'Please,' Angie scoffed. 'Do you know how many men have said that to me? And all of them wanted to get in my pants.'

'Well, I've already been in your pants, so you'll have to take the compliment.'

Angie pressed her head into the pillow and tried to hide her smile. 'We should replenish our energy. I still have some cookies upstairs.'

Liam planted a kiss on Angie's cheek. 'Sounds amazing.'

'I'm happy to have turned this birthday around for you,' she said. 'Kind of like how you turned mine around earlier in the year.'

'Turned it around?' Liam grinned and embraced her in a cuddle. 'It's the best birthday I've ever had.'

Upstairs, Angie flicked the switch on the kettle. Strong hands wrapped around her body from behind. A warmth erupted in her belly and dispersed through her entire body.

'These are good cookies,' Liam said as he took a bite of the chocolate chip dough.

Angie smiled as she put a teabag into each mug.

This was bliss. This was what a relationship was supposed to be like. No pretending. No fear. Right now, she was allowed, able to be herself.

'Did you see that?' Liam stiffened. 'I saw headlights through the windows.'

'Probably the neighbours. And I don't care about them. But I do care about another kiss.' Angie turned around. As she was about to kiss

Liam's lips, the doorbell rang, making her jump.

'What the?' Angie glanced at Liam. 'Who'd be knocking on the door at this time?' Angie switched off the kettle and headed for the front door.

Who the hell could it be? When she opened the door, reality kicked her in the stomach. Her real life had returned. It was no longer a distant, intangible memory.

'Babe, I'm so happy to see you.' The man dropped a duffel bag at the door and leaned in to wrap his arms around her shoulders.

It took Angie a moment to muster something, anything.

'Michael,' she whispered. Her arms stayed limp beside her body as his arms closed in around her shoulders.

'What're you doing here?'

The touch of his body on hers wasn't welcome and sent a cold shiver across her skin. Only a week ago he'd told her he was leaving their marriage, and now he was on the doorstep of her holiday house pretending nothing had happened.

Michael pulled away and smiled as he brushed a piece of hair off her face.

Something was off about him. His eyes, the way he smelled. Michael's aura wasn't the same as when he left. Something wasn't right.

'I'm so sorry for everything, Angie. I made a mistake. Let's go home.'

BIRTHDAY WISH

Book three

HER BIRTHDAY WISH IS IN HIS HANDS

CHAPTER ONE

'Sign here. And here. Oh, and here. That's why I put the stickers there. Need to make sure you sign in all the right places before you leave today.' Catherine, the lawyer, smiled as she watched Liam sign his life away on the craziest thing he'd done so far in his life.

Liam kept his eyes on her slim fingers and long red fingernails as she pointed to the places he needed to sign.

Once the last flick of the pen left the page, a heavy weight lifted off Liam's shoulders. A breath released from deep within his lungs, and he looked up at the woman and smiled.

She took the papers and straightened them against the desk before placing them in a purple tray filled to the brim with documents.

'Congratulations, Liam. It's official. You're now the proud part-owner of the hottest new bar in Canberra, along with Jaxon Thomas. I wish you all the success in the world.' She stood up, revealing an exceptionally tight black pencil skirt and a cream blouse that showed off a pink lacy lavender bra beneath.

It made Liam's heart beat a little faster.

Catherine's dainty, classic beauty was startling.

Liam knew right away she was the right woman to help draw up the contract for the new bar. She oozed professionalism and took the time to explain everything to him in a way he understood.

It was a relief when Catherine stepped into the waiting area when he arrived at the law firm for his first appointment. He was perspiring, his hands clammy and jaw tight, hoping to heaven the woman he loved didn't appear in the waiting room. Even after spending a passionate week in the Gumtree Plains with Angie, he hadn't seen or spoken to her in months.

Catherine's slicked back brunette ponytail and large frame glasses emphasised her angular features and large brown eyes. In a way, she reminded him of Angie.

Angie.

The woman who haunted his dreams. He hated walking through life with everything reminding him of her sweet smile and the hint of her floral perfume. Even this young woman, who looked nothing like Angie, reminded him of her laugh, the way she smelled after a shower, and the giggle she made when he said something funny.

Why wouldn't the memory of her leave him alone?

'Thanks, Catherine. I really appreciate you taking the time to walk me through the process and explaining it all to me. I'm a bit of a legal dummy,' he said as he raised his hands in mock surrender.

Catherine's face flushed pink. His own face flushed hot in reaction. Sometimes he forgot his impact on women.

'Call me anytime if you need legal advice or have any questions. Otherwise, best of luck.' She offered him her hand.

They stood there, shaking hands for longer than necessary, but it was nice to meet a down-to-earth woman. Liam had sworn off dating since the week he'd spent with Angie at Christmastime.

Even though it'd been almost four months, he was still trying to heal his busted heart. A heart badly bruised from what went down. Namely, her husband returning with an announcement that he wanted her back.

When Liam looked in Angie's eyes that night, there was something in them he'd never noticed before. Fear? Indecision? Liam got the feeling she didn't want to go back to her husband. But they were married. Marriage meant something to her, and Liam wasn't going to argue with her decision.

'This might sound forward, so feel free to put me in my place, but the opening of the bar is tonight. I'll shout you a drink if you head on down. No pressure at all. But it should be fun. Discounted drinks and a live band.'

Catherine didn't pull her hand away from Liam's. Instead, they continued to stand there, shaking hands and smiling.

'Are you asking me on a date, Liam?'

'Not at all. I'm guessing there's some lawyer-client code that says you can't. But it's a free drink. And I'll even put out a bowl of chips for you,' he said with a mock wink.

'Well, technically our working relationship is over. I'm attending a ball tonight, but maybe I'll head on over after that, I can even bring some people and introduce them to the hottest new bar in Canberra. Us lawyers do like to let our hair down occasionally.'

Liam smiled, a rare occurrence for him these days. 'I'll be there all night so stop by anytime.'

'Perfect,' Catherine replied.

* * *

'All signed, mate? Took you bloody long enough. Now you're really stuck with me.'

'I guess I am, Jax,' Liam said as he hit the accelerator when the light turned green at the intersection.

After Christmas, Liam did some soul searching. Without Angie, he was looking for his place in the world. Angie was home, the woman he wanted to be with. But fate didn't feel the same way.

He came back to Canberra as single as when he left. Sitting at his desk at work, his mind wouldn't allow him to forget. It kept bringing up memories, reminders of their time together in Gumtree Plains. That one moment when they were one. He'd never been so damn happy in his life as when he was with Angie, lying in bed and drawing circles on her naked skin as she smiled back at him.

Coming back to his desk and staring at the computer screen at work reminded him how much he hated his job. Knowing he and Angie were over for good, he wondered what would come of his life if he never took a chance. People wouldn't remember him as the guy who played it safe. He wanted to do something that would make him proud.

After months of sweet talking and persuasion, Liam finally called Jax back and told him he was *in*.

'Are you sure about the name? I mean, *Cowboys* is a bit lame don't you think?'

'Ahh,' Liam said as he pressed down the indicator and took the last turn into the city. 'It's a bit late for that now, mate. Name's been registered. Marketing's got the name written all over it. What, are you getting cold feet?' Liam asked.

'Nah, I just want this to be a success. I *really* want to be able to hand in my resignation at the end of the year and do this thing full-time.'

'You and me both,' Liam replied. The only thing was Liam had already quit his job. The secret was being kept under wraps for now. Not even Mum and Dad knew. Liam was invested one hundred percent in this bar. It couldn't fail, or his life savings would go down the drain with it.

'So, you've got the staffing roster sorted?' Liam asked. 'Remember, we're going to need a couple more people given it's opening night.'

'All sorted, mate. Waiting for you to get here so we can start the briefing and do the final checks.'

Liam pulled into the car park in the alleyway behind the bar. Once he got out, he headed towards his new job. A new life. A new future.

It tore at his heart realising he would never be able to share this with Angie. But he couldn't dwell on that now. Each step he took towards the bar was a step closer to his new life.

A jolt of excitement pumped through his veins as he approached the next chapter. Finally, Liam had something to live for again. He had purpose. Something to work towards.

Cowboys was Liam's future. Angie was his past.

CHAPTER TWO

The lights glared bright, almost blinding her, and Angie resisted the urge to hold her hand up to her forehead and get a better look out over the sea of people.

Music blared in the background, but she couldn't figure out what the song was. She was too busy trying not to fall over in the ridiculous sky-high heels Lizzie had pressured her into buying. Sure, they made her look tall and elegant, but they were as tricky as walking a trapeze.

When she reached the stage, Angie pulled up the front of her dress as she climbed the steps, and the blue and grey sequins tickled the skin of her fingers. As she strolled across the stage to the microphone, she tried not to think about all eyes in the audience watching her every move.

'Congratulations, Angela. This is such a well-deserved win.' Her boss shook her hand and passed her the trophy.

Angie wasn't normally a hugger, but on this occasion, she couldn't help it. She wrapped her arms around George, the senior partner at her firm, and held the tears in check. His burly arms hugged her back in the Giorgio Armani suit covering his large frame.

'Thank you so much, George. I couldn't have done any of this without you.' When she pulled away from him, she spotted the sparkle in his eye and he quickly wiped away the tears.

George had been her mentor since she'd started at the firm as a bright and starry-eyed twenty-two-year-old, and he'd always supported her endeavours and dreams to become the best lawyer she could.

Now, Angie saw him more as a father figure who protected her and always had her back. And she knew of the special spot she held in his heart too.

George stepped out of the light, receding into the shadows, and left Angie in the middle of the stage by herself. She normally hated being the centre of attention, but tonight was an exception. Being recognised as one of the rising talents in her firm was a tribute to all the long hours in the office and hard work she'd dedicated to her clients, especially the most vulnerable clients.

The music faded and she was left standing in a still room under bright lights. All that could be heard from the audience was the odd cough. She stepped closer to the microphone and took a deep breath.

'Wow, I have no words,' she began, holding back the tears and hoping it didn't smudge her mascara. Her hands shook as she tried to get the words out. So many things ran through her mind. So many people to thank. She took another deep breath and tried to gather her thoughts so she could sound somewhat eloquent.

'I've spent a long time in this firm. Not as long as some, but I've certainly spent many years in a place I've come to love. Almost seven years to be exact. I couldn't imagine being anywhere else.' She spoke of her time as a young lawyer trying to make her way up the ranks in a gig that was tougher than she could've imagined. Waves of emotion overcame her and she couldn't contain the tears any longer.

'I'm sorry,' she blubbered in front of the audience.

George appeared behind her and handed her a tissue from his pocket.

Reliable George. Always there to save the day.

Angie took the tissue from George and then he disappeared into the shadows again. 'There are so many people I have to thank. George, thank you for being my mentor. I remember when I walked into the firm on my first day and you told me this job wasn't for the faint of heart and I had to be tough. I didn't know if I was cut out for it and considered walking out and never coming back. But I've carried those words with me to this day and realise you were preparing me for the toughest and most rewarding job of my life. To my wonderful friend, Lizzie, who has worked beside me on some seriously challenging cases. It took many late nights full of pizza and fizzy drinks to meet our deadlines, but we did it. Thank you to my parents who have done nothing but support me in my dreams to follow in their footsteps, and letting me live at home as I transitioned from a junior to a senior lawyer so I could save for a deposit on my own place. My colleagues.

You make the work day seem not so long. And finally, I want to dedicate this award to my clients. The beautiful people I meet each day who put their trust in me to get them out of some hairy situations. The clients who trust me to fight for them when they can't fight for themselves. Thank you for giving me purpose. This one's for you. Thank you.'

Angie wiped the last tear off her face with the tissue and held it in the palm of her hand. The crowd roared into applause and an upbeat song thumped in the background.

Carefully, she stepped down the stairs and headed back to the table in the middle of the room. Winning this award was a dream come true. Each year, Angie had attended the awards ceremony and wished one day she'd earn such a prestigious accolade. She placed the trophy on the table and smiled at it.

'Congratulations, babe.' Lizzie stood up and hugged her tight.

'Thank you,' she breathed into Lizzie's ear.

Mum and Dad smiled from across the table. They weren't big on emotions, but she knew they were immensely proud of their only child.

As she took her seat, Michael placed his hand on hers. But instead of holding it delicately like he normally did, he squeezed it uncomfortably tight. Angie jolted at the pressure and tried to pull her hand away.

The crowd cheered as another person was called to the stage to receive an award.

'I can't believe the nerve of you up there,' he whispered in her ear through gritted teeth.

Angie tried to pull free, but he wouldn't let go of her hand. He didn't need to say the words. It was clear by the strength of his grip, and the smugness spread across his face, that he was pissed off.

But Angie had no regrets. If she had her time up on stage again, she'd do the same damn thing. After the cheating saga, the lying, the inability to take responsibility for anything he'd done, he didn't deserve any acknowledgment in her acceptance speech for which she had worked so hard to achieve on her own.

Angie finally ripped her hand free from his grip and grabbed the glass of white wine next to her plate, allowing the chilly liquid to cool her hand. She managed to keep herself composed, but on the inside, her beating heart pulsed at an alarming rate.

Michael had ruined her chances with Liam. And he'd ruined her marriage when he left her a week before Christmas for some bimbo on the beach in Hawaii. The last thing she was going to let him do was ruin her night after winning the most important award of her career.

CHAPTER THREE

'Rosemary's vomiting in the bathroom.'

Liam lifted his head from the bar where he was mixing a Pina Colada. The music was booming and it was only ten p.m.

Amanda, one of the young staff members, was standing in front of Liam holding a tray of drinks. Her body was stiff and her expression blank.

'Is she okay?' he asked, not quite sure what to do. He'd been an employee his whole life. Managing staff, and apparently their illnesses, was unfamiliar territory.

'I don't think so. Can you go in there and check on her?'

Liam looked across at Jax who was simultaneously taking a payment behind the bar, and chatting up two blondes in short black dresses and cowgirl boots.

'I don't think that's appropriate, Amanda. I can't really go into the women's bathroom. How about I take that tray and you take her out back to the office. I'll bring in a bucket for her and call her next of kin.' This was exactly what he didn't need on the opening night of *Cowboys*.

'Please, Liam. She won't come out. I think she's really sick. And I've got three back orders to get through that I didn't write down.'

Liam resisted an eye roll. He'd told Amanda earlier in the night to write down the damn orders in case something like this happened.

'Okay. Keep doing what you're doing. You're doing a great job by the way.' Liam grabbed the cleaning sign from behind the bar.

Outside the women's bathroom, he opened the door and called out, 'Hello?' He wasn't going to enter the bathroom if he didn't have to, and he certainly wasn't going to step foot inside if the cubicles were occupied.

As he was about to go in, the door swung open and two women emerged, eyeballing him up and down.

'Hi, handsome.'

'Evening, ladies,' he said, trying to remain cool but focusing on the task at hand.

'Fancy a drink?' The brunette said as she ran her index finger along his chest and over his bicep. The touch of the woman's fingernail left a trail of goose bumps on his skin. The last time a woman had touched him was ...

Liam smiled. He didn't hate the attention from women, but since Angie, he'd lost all interest in brief flings. 'Maybe later. Right now, I have to save someone.'

'I'll hold you to it,' the woman said with a wink as she stepped away, followed by her friend.

Liam nodded politely. The sign dropped on the ground to signal the bathroom was closed.

'Hello?' he called out.

No one answered. The coast was clear. As he neared the last bay, vomiting sounds filled the airwaves. His stomach churned like a washing machine.

'Rosemary? It's Liam. You alright?'

'I'm okay,' the young woman replied through gasping breaths. 'I promise I'm not drunk. I think I have food poisoning.'

The sounds of her dry retching in the bathroom continued, bouncing off the tiles and echoing throughout the entire toilet block.

What he wanted to do was run away. He'd had a fear of vomit his entire life, but he couldn't exactly leave his employee vomiting in the bathroom on opening night. Even as a child vomit made him sick to his stomach. But Mum would've killed him if he didn't help a woman in need.

'Rosemary, I'm coming into the bathroom now to help you. Is that okay?'

She didn't respond.

When he reached the last bay, he pushed the door open. Rosemary was on her knees. Her hands were clutched around the toilet bowl and her tiny body heaved inside it.

'Rosemary, is there someone I can call to come pick you up?'

'Tim. My roommate. He'll come get me.'

'Do you have his number?'

She pulled a phone from her pocket and pressed her arm behind her body in an awkward position to hand it to him.

Liam was much closer to the smell now. His stomach tightened as bile shot up his throat. He turned on his heels, rushed to the sink and dry retched.

Come on man, hold it together.

Taking one deep breath, he looked up at the mirror. When he'd signed up to co-own a bar, he didn't realise he'd have to deal with a hairy situation like this.

He swung back around, took the phone from Rosemary and made the call.

'Tim will be here in fifteen minutes. I think the best thing to do at this point is to get you into the office with a bucket. At least you can sit down where it's warm.'

Rosemary slid onto her behind with her back against the toilet. She stared up at Liam and smiled. 'You're a sweet guy,' she said as she wiped her mouth with the back of her hand. 'I knew I shouldn't have eaten that sushi for lunch.'

'There's your problem. I couldn't think of anything worse than sushi. Sounds a bit fishy to me.' It was a lame attempt at a joke, but he got a smile.

'Come on, let's get you out of here.' Liam offered his hand and pulled her to her feet. But instead of standing on her own, her legs folded like jelly, and she fell into Liam's chest and threw up once more, covering his new black polo shirt with vomit.

Oh my God!

The urge to push her off and rip the shirt off to wash it under the tap was overwhelming, but he couldn't drop Rosemary on the tiles. The girl could barely stand.

Her brown eyes grew wide. 'Liam, I'm so sorry,' she apologised as she wiped her mouth again. 'Please don't fire me.'

Liam held her at arms-length to ensure she stayed on her feet. 'You're not fired, Rosemary,' he said as he hooked his arm behind her back and underneath her armpit.

It took all his strength to not vomit himself with the bitter stench permeating through the bathroom, and now on his clothes.

In the office, he grabbed a bucket and placed it between her legs. 'It should only be ten minutes now. I'll let you know when Tim gets here. If you need anything, use the phone to call me at the bar.' He pointed to the phone at the edge of the desk.

Liam went to leave the office when Rosemary called out to him. 'Thanks for looking after me, boss. Appreciate it.'

Liam feigned a smile. It seemed ridiculous, and a little disgusting, that he was standing in his office wearing a polo shirt covered in someone else's vomit. But this was the life he'd chosen. He was now a boss and businessman. Without another job to go back to, he didn't have a choice. He was going to make this work, even if it killed him. And that meant getting his hands dirty. Literally.

'You're welcome, Rosemary. Sit tight.' With that, he left the office. Heading for the ladies bathroom, he didn't know what was worse: being covered in someone else's vomit, or having to clean it up.

'Dear Lord, please don't let anymore drama happen tonight,' he mumbled under his breath as he pulled the mop from the bucket and began cleaning the bathroom.

CHAPTER FOUR

'Come on, Ange. Let's go out,' Lizzie whined as she hooked her arm through Angie's.

They were walking across the manicured gardens of the five-star hotel to their parked cars.

'It's a school night, Lizzie. And we have a big day in court tomorrow,' Angie said as they teetered across the bitumen in their high heels.

For an April night in Canberra, the temperature was surprisingly balmy. It lifted Angie's spirits a little knowing they might get a few more warm nights before the cold set in.

'Angie, I love you, but you can be so boring sometimes,' Lizzie complained as she pulled her arm away to try and balance herself on the uneven concrete.

'I think it's time we head home,' Angie replied.

'But Ange—'

'Elizabeth, shut up. Angie's not interested, so we're not going out, okay?' Michael snapped.

Angie stopped in the middle of the manicured garden next to a green hedge underneath a lamp post, and stared at Michael as he walked ahead, his eyes locked to the screen of his smartphone. The prick didn't even have the decency to look at them when he insulted her best friend.

It was one thing Angie telling Lizzie off, but Michael didn't have the right. Who the hell did he think he was speaking to her friend like that?

'Mate, come on. Now's not the time or the place.' Eli, Lizzie's friend, said as the three of them stood next to the hedge in their cocktail outfits.

Michael turned around and finally lifted his eyes from his smartphone to look at them. 'Not you too, Eli.'

Angie's eyes narrowed and her hands tightened into a fist. Who was this man standing in front of her? She didn't even know her own husband anymore.

I don't think I ever knew him.

It still perplexed her everyday why Michael asked her to stay to give their marriage six more months. To see if they could work out their differences. But trying to regain her trust after Michael's infidelity was a daily challenge. Some days, it seemed like he wasn't even trying.

'She's sloshed. Take her home. The last thing she should be doing is getting hammered tonight,' Michael argued.

Under the light of the lamp post, Angie turned to Lizzie and said, 'I think we should go out for one drink. Where do you want to go?'

Lizzie punched her hand in the air. 'There's the wing woman I know and love. Let's get the hell out of here.' Lizzie grabbed Angie and Eli's hands and they passed Michael, leaving him with his smartphone.

It was minuscule payback compared to what Michael had done, But it was payback nonetheless.

* * *

'What is this place?' Angie asked as they stepped inside a warm, bustling bar.

It was unlike any place she'd ever been before. The bar and floorboards were polished oak and there was a fireplace in the corner of the room, generating the kind of warmth only wood could provide.

A band played on a raised stage with banjos and drums, and the bar had several lines of people waiting to be served.

A young woman approached them in a white shirt with rolled up sleeves, ripped bootleg jeans and cowgirl boots. 'Welcome to *Cowboys*. Do you guys want a table?'

'Yes!' Lizzie replied, barely able to contain her excitement. 'Do you have one by the fireplace?'

'Sure do. Follow me,' the young woman said.

Angie followed Lizzie and Eli to the other side of the bar. Lizzie's arm was linked through Eli's and they chatted away like best friends. The two were a perfect pair with Eli in a grey tuxedo and Lizzie's off-the-shoulder, raven red floor-length dress.

The years of lifting weights had given Lizzie a sculpted figure, and the dress looked sensational clinging to her toned body.

Angie had always wondered why Lizzie and Eli never got together. They seemed like the perfect fit. Lizzie was outgoing and enthusiastic, while Eli was a little more reserved. He took care of her like a boyfriend should. But every time Angie suggested he could be more than a friend, Lizzie brushed it off.

Angie tucked the clutch under her arm when someone grabbed her wrist.

'What the hell do you think you're doing?' The flames from the fireplace flickered like a raging bushfire in Michael's hazel eyes.

'What am *I* doing? Having some damn fun. Kind of like what you did when you went to Hawaii, only I'm not fucking someone else.' Angie drew in a sharp breath, surprised by her own comment.

Cursing wasn't something she did often, but when she did, it was for good reason. 'And if you don't let go of my wrist,' she continued. 'I'll sure as hell be bringing this up in the divorce proceedings. Don't you dare try and man handle me like I'm a wild animal.'

Michael let go of her wrist. 'We're not getting a divorce,' he said through gritted teeth.

The back and forth was exhausting. Angie couldn't pinpoint why he was still holding onto their marriage, yet treating her with such indifference.

After a moment, his face softened and his shoulders relaxed. 'I'm sorry. I think I've had a bit too much to drink.'

They stood in the middle of the country themed bar in their cocktail outfits. While the sequins on Angie's dress glittered under the light, Michael's tuxedo and black bow tie made him look like a pompous jerk.

'I promised you four months to try this thing and it's been a living hell. Who do you think you are getting physical with me? Telling my friends off? I'm so disappointed in you, Michael. I can't even look at you right now.' Angie pushed past him and headed to the table where Lizzie and Eli were sitting in the corner of the bar, swaying to the tunes of the live band.

Since that night with Liam in Gumtree Plains, Angie had spent many nights lying awake in Michael's penthouse, wondering if she loved her husband anymore. At first, it was lust, passion, awe for his success. She'd be lying if she said she wasn't wooed by his wealth either. But love? These last few months had been a true test of whether she could forgive and forget what he'd done.

Can we ever go back to the way things were?

She wasn't sure.

A tear streamed down her face and she swiped it away quickly with the back of her hand. How did her life come to this? Stuck in a loveless marriage and pining for a man she could never have.

Liam would probably never forgive her for leaving. Not a second time. And if he never forgave her, she'd understand. That didn't mean she didn't miss him like crazy. Her heart ached for him, yearned for his embrace. Every day she lived with regret for not choosing him.

When Michael had showed up at the holiday house in Gumtree Plains unannounced at Christmas, Angie had fought the urge to punch him. Kick him. Physically injure him so he could at least experience some of the pain he'd put her through.

Looking at him now made her skin crawl like she was covered in millions of spiders. Her body reacted the opposite way to how she thought she'd feel. There was no way she could stay with him after he'd cheated. And yet, here they were, pretending to be a happy couple in front of their friends.

Michael had begged, apologised. He'd even cried, pulling out all the manipulation tactics, saying the right things to tug at her heartstrings. Yet he had destroyed her trust. He begged for another six months to try again. Angie didn't want to. Her heart had already been taken by another.

But she *was* married to Michael. They were tied together by vows and promises. Marriage was sacred. If she didn't at least try, she would never forgive herself.

Angie sat down at the corner booth and placed the clutch in her lap.

Lizzie grabbed Angie's hand and leaned towards her. 'I don't want to alarm you, but there's someone here that we know.'

'Well, it is Canberra. Can't go anywhere without seeing someone you know in this town.'

'I'm serious, Ange.' Lizzie paused. 'It's Liam. He's behind the bar and he's talking to Catherine.'

Angie's entire body froze. Liam couldn't be in the same bar on the same night. Could he? Angie swallowed and slowly looked over her shoulder towards the bar. It was him alright. The sight of his face, his muscled body hidden under that fitted polo shirt, made her palms slick with sweat.

The thudding of her heart rang loud in her ears as she watched him talk to Catherine, an old...acquaintance from university.

Angie whipped back around. 'What's he doing here?'

Lizzie shrugged. 'I don't know. Are you going to talk to him?'

Angie looked back over her shoulder. She hadn't spoken to him in four months, not since the night they'd made love.

The night she broke his heart.

Liam looked even more gorgeous than she remembered. His tanned skin glistened under the lights at the bar, and his dark stubble had grown a little longer, making him look older than his age. There was a rugged aura about him, something more mature. But there was also a hardness about him. His face was no longer the soft, smiling face she'd come to love. The slight lines in his forehead and tiny wrinkles at the corners of his eyes told her he wasn't the same man.

Michael finally sat down next to them, his eyes glued to his smartphone. He was posting about what a great night he'd had on social media.

Oh, please!

She couldn't stand it anymore. Without casting another thought to the consequences, Angie stood up and headed to the bar.

CHAPTER FIVE

'You made it,' Liam said when he looked up and Catherine was standing by the bar.

'What a great turnout,' she replied as she looked around the place.

Cowboys was different to the other nightspots and Liam hoped the casual, laid back vibe would work in his favour.

Catherine looked even more stunning than she had earlier in the day at her office. The black dress hugged every curve and plunged deep between her breasts, revealing enough cleavage to make him wonder what they'd feel like in his hands.

Her brunette hair was parted at the side and flowed in long waves past her shoulders. The smoky eye makeup and red lipstick amplified her angular features, showing off her natural, delicate beauty.

Maybe there was someone out there who could get the blood pumping through his veins again.

'You've done well for yourself,' she said as she leaned over the bar, getting closer to him. She stopped halfway and sniffed the air. 'Do you smell that?'

Shit.

Liam hadn't had time to change his shirt. 'Oh, nothing. Someone had an accident and I had to clean it up. Food poisoning, I think.'

Catherine leaned back.

'What're we drinking tonight?' he asked, quickly changing the subject.

'Surprise me,' she said as she leaned into the bar once more. Her cleavage was exposed and it made Liam swallow, hard.

A smile crept up the corner of Catherine's mouth as she stared at him with longing brown eyes.

Was she coming onto him? He'd forgotten how to flirt with women, so he wasn't sure. 'Coming right up,' he said as he slipped out the back to the office.

He pulled off the polo shirt and shoved it into a plastic bag. There was a spare shirt sitting on the back of the chair. As he pulled it over his muscled shoulders, it was a bit too snug around his body. But he didn't have any other options at this point. He'd rather a small shirt to one that smelled like vomit.

Stepping back out onto the floor behind the bar, Catherine was talking to another woman in a dress. She must've been at the same event Catherine attended tonight.

He got to work making a cocktail of Malibu, Vodka and orange. After he'd shaken, stirred and poured the cocktail, he placed a tiny umbrella in the glass and popped it on the bar in front of Catherine.

'You're too good. Thank you.' Without breaking eye contact, she brushed past him to reach for a short straw.

Could he get lost in those eyes the way he did with Angie?

'Hello, Liam.'

Liam looked at the woman standing next to Catherine. It took a moment for him to recognise her. Then his heart rate surged. The swirling in his belly almost brought him to his knees. He didn't have to wonder whether he'd get lost in another woman's eyes with Angie standing right in front of him.

'Liam, this is Angie. We went to law school together. We were the two most competitive women in our cohort,' Catherine announced as she gently jabbed Angie in the arm before sipping from the cocktail.

Angie didn't move. Her eyes were fixed on Liam. Her dress was a little more conservative than Catherine's. The high neckline covered her cleavage, but Liam didn't forget their warmth and roundness beneath his hands when he'd caressed her breasts as they were making love.

The blue and grey sequins sparkled and glowed under the lights, just like Angie's personality. Her blonde hair was longer now and pulled into a high bun. There were strands of blonde, curled hair, falling past her cheeks.

Cheeks he'd kissed.

Cheeks he was certain he'd never kiss again.

'Do you two know each other?' Catherine asked, as she looked between them.

Angie blinked a couple of times. Then she turned and walked away, leaving the bar. Liam was sure he'd imagined it. Seeing Angie in his bar was a dream come true and a nightmare at the same time.

Why was she running away from him when all he wanted to do was run toward her and take her in his arms?

Catherine sipped her cocktail. 'Well, that was stran—'

'Excuse me.' Liam walked out from behind the bar and followed Angie as she weaved through the groups of people in *Cowboys*.

It was a moment to celebrate. It was a success people had turned up to opening night and were enjoying the atmosphere. But all Liam cared about was chasing Angie to find out why she was running away.

As soon as he reached her, he regretted following her footsteps. Lizzie was sitting in the booth with another man. And then Liam locked eyes with...him.

Michael looked up at them both. For a moment, he seemed confused. Then he stood up with a tense jaw and tight fists. 'What the fuck is *he* doing here?' Michael demanded, pointing in Liam's direction.

Liam looked between Angie and Michael, equally as surprised by the situation.

How could she have married this jerk?

'Actually, I'm the—'

'The what? The lowly barman who fucked my wife while I was overseas working? Listen, mate. You'd better get out of my face before I beat the shit out of you.'

'Oh really?' Liam replied. 'A scrawny little man like you is going to beat the shit out of *me*?' Liam's chest puffed out and he took a step towards Michael so they were face-to-face.

He wasn't backing down, the same way he'd done the day Michael had turned up to Gumtree Plains unannounced and ruined Liam's perfect Christmas with Angie.

'Yeah, really.' Michael pulled off his suit jacket, dropped it on the table, then he threw a swing at Liam.

Liam ducked, and held his hand out, keeping Michael at arm's length.

Michael had nothing on Liam. He could've easily won a fight, but he refused to throw a punch on opening night. His bar was supposed to be a peaceful place for a drink with friends.

'Jax! Call security!' Liam yelled across the bar as he fended off the husband of the woman he loved.

Michael continued to throw punches and managed to clip Liam's chin. But Liam stood his ground. There'd be no fights in this bar tonight.

'On it!' Jax called out.

Within seconds, security arrived and grabbed Michael by the arms, dragging him out of the bar as he yelled profanities in Liam's direction.

The chatter in the bar disappeared, replaced only by the soft strums of the country song the band was playing on stage.

Liam turned back to Angie.

Her eyes were wide. She slumped into the booth seat next to Lizzie.

'Angie, I'm sorry. I didn't mean for that to happen.'

Angie leaned into Lizzie, and Lizzie wrapped her arm around her shoulders. 'I can't say he didn't deserve it.' Angie didn't seem her normal self. Her arms were thinner, her cheeks more sunken. Darker circles under her eyes.

Looking in her eyes, Liam could see something was missing. An emptiness. Liam didn't blame her with a husband like Michael.

He stood in front of Angie and her friends, not sure what to say. What could he say? The last time he'd seen her, they'd had a magical evening of making love.

When Michael showed up, the two men got into a scuffle and Liam left of his own accord. The only things he'd heard about Angie were through his sister-in-law, Jen since they became friends.

Did he deserve an explanation as to why she was still with her husband? Maybe. But tonight wasn't the night to ask.

So instead of asking why, Liam turned around and walked back to his bar.

CHAPTER SIX

The key clicked as Angie turned it in the door around eleven p.m. She hoped Michael had fallen asleep and she didn't have to put up with another fight. The last four months had been completely draining.

She was trying, she really was. But she was beginning to question whether this marriage would last, or she was simply flogging a dead horse.

As the door opened, she was greeted by the generously sized penthouse high above Canberra's Foreshore. It was a two-story, three-bedroom penthouse with a large balcony, chef's kitchen, theatre and gym. It was more than two people could ever need, but Michael was never satisfied with the bare necessities.

As she made her way to the kitchen, the lamp in the living room switched on. Angie jolted and dropped her clutch on the tiles.

'Where have you been?'

'Jesus, Michael.' She pressed her hands against her furiously beating heart. 'I was out.'

'With him?'

Angie stared at Michael. She didn't owe him an explanation. Not after everything he'd put her through.

'Get off your high horse,' she said as she picked her clutch off the tiles and headed to the bedroom. 'I'm allowed to go out with friends. And tonight was a special occasion.'

'Pathetic,' he said before sipping whiskey from a crystal glass.

Angie stopped and turned to stare at him. '*I'm* pathetic? *I* didn't do anything wrong.'

'And I did? I was man-handled in that dump and thrown outside like a bag of trash. You didn't even check if I was okay. I could've been seriously injured by those baboons.'

It was true. She didn't check on him. On purpose. Associating with Michael's self-entitled behaviour was a liability.

Angie dropped her clutch on the marble bench in the kitchen. 'By the looks of it, you're fine. And besides, you threw a punch at someone. You're the one guilty of potential battery and acting like a total brat. Do you realise how stupid it was to try and punch him in public? He could press charges against you. Someone could've got your little outburst on camera!'

Michael sighed and tipped the glass from side-to-side in his hand. 'I was standing up for myself. For us. I only threw a punch at him because he took advantage of you.'

'You dumped me for a bimbo when you were in Hawaii at Christmastime. He never took advantage of me. I was a willing participant.'

And I regret nothing.

Michael closed his eyes and tilted his head back. He placed the glass on the coffee table beside the recliner and stood up. 'Are you going to crucify me until the end of time? I don't know how many times I can apologise for my mistake.'

Angie crossed her arms. The chill of the autumn night had finally caught up with her, making her skin rise with goose bumps.

'I'm struggling, Michael.'

'I know you are. But you can't keep bringing up stuff from the past. I've already forgiven you for your little...indiscretion.' He walked towards her slowly, across the tiles of the apartment.

He made it sound like she was the one who had an affair, who'd betrayed his trust.

'I don't know if I'll ever get over what you did. You stood me up and dumped me over the phone.'

Only a coward would do that.

'But I came back to you,' he argued. When he reached her, he ran his hands down her slender arms. Arms that had lost weight since she'd decided to stay by her husband's side.

It didn't feel right. In the pit of her stomach, a knot tightened with each day that went by. She didn't want to give up on this marriage. Surely, she could learn to love him again. Couldn't she?

And he was right. She'd slept with Liam while they were still married. Maybe she was just as bad as Michael.

Michael's hands moved from her arms to her back, and over her behind. The same electricity that Liam sent through her body when he touched her didn't exist with Michael.

'Michael—'

'Angie, we haven't had sex since I left for Hawaii. Can't we at least try?'

It seemed unnatural, forced from his end. Even as he kept his hands on her body, he still maintained distance between them.

Did he really want to make love to her, or did he only want sex for the sake of it?

The whole situation was screwing with her head. The last time she had sex was with... 'How about we take it one step at a time,' she offered as she placed her hands on his and gently pushed them off her body.

'When will you get over this?' Michael's voice rose, reminding her of the way he'd grabbed her hand uncomfortably earlier in the night.

'It's not that simple. I can't turn my body on and off like a tap.' What she needed was love. And tenderness. A little foreplay never went astray either. Michael always insisted on getting to the main course straight up.

'I don't know how much longer I can do this,' she admitted.

'What?'

'This marriage.'

They stared at each other. Michael's cleanly shaved face made him look more like a sixteen-year-old than a man of thirty-six. The bow tie was undone and hanging around his neck, and the scent of whiskey permeated his breath.

'I love you, Angie. More than anything in this world. I told you I made a mistake. It's why I came back to you.' He took her hands in his and squeezed them. 'We can't throw away this marriage. Not after only a few months. Don't you want to try?'

The honest answer was she didn't know. What would happen when he found someone younger again? Sexier? Then what? And if she searched deep inside her soul, she knew her heart didn't belong to him anymore.

'I'm tired. I'm going to bed.'

'Fine,' Michael whined. 'I have to make a phone call anyway,' he said as he turned away from her and headed towards the study.

'At this time of night?' Angie questioned as she glanced at the clock in the kitchen.

He ignored her as he stepped into the study and slammed the door behind him.

* * *

The alarm buzzed on Angie's phone. Her eyes fluttered open as they adjusted to the light filtering into the room from outside.

She picked up the phone and saw a message from Jen, Liam's sister-in-law. They'd stayed in contact since her week in the Snowy Mountains. Jen had become a confidant, and was due to have her baby any week now.

I'll be in Canberra next weekend for my baby shower. Would love for you to come. My friend will send details via email soon. Feel free to bring a plus one!

Angie rolled over in bed. Michael was fast asleep at the other side of the king size mattress. Having such a large bed allowed them to sleep on opposite sides, never having to touch one another. It was the way they'd been sleeping since they'd returned to Canberra.

She looked back at her phone. It was a sweet invitation, but she wasn't sure she'd accept. Things were messy. Seeing Liam last night was like seeing a ghost. It was terrifying and exhilarating at the same time. She wanted to escape his presence, yet for him to hold her in his arms.

Michael rolled over and threw his arm over her body. He wriggled himself towards her and his erection poked her in the hip.

'Come on, babe,' he said as he began caressing her breasts, still half-asleep. 'Let me put it in, just for a minute.'

At that very moment, Angie's alarm sounded again. She threw the doona offer her legs and made her way to the bathroom. 'Sorry. I have to get ready for work.'

* * *

'What did you say to Michael when you got home?' Lizzie whispered as they stepped into court for a full morning of hearings.

'I told him the truth, that I'm struggling,' Angie replied as they stepped into the courtroom and bowed to the Australian crest behind the Judge's chair. They approached the solicitors' tables and sat down. Angie began preparing her papers.

'Are you alright about seeing Liam last night? I mean, talk about awkward,' Lizzie said before she applied a layer of lipstick in front of a hand-held mirror.

'You can say that again.' Angie had rehearsed a thousand times what she'd say to Liam if she saw him again. That was thrown out the window when she saw him in the flesh.

Would she ever get over him? She didn't know if she could. And now that she knew where he worked, she was going to have to make an effort to stay away.

'You're at four months now with Michael. Do you think you'll separate?' Lizzie asked as she snapped the hand-held mirror shut and dropped it in her handbag.

'I—'

'Good morning.'

Angie and Lizzie both turned to greet the meek voice behind them.

'Julie, how are you today?' Angie said as she stood up from behind the desk to meet her client.

She was thankful for the convenient interruption. She wasn't ready to answer Lizzie's question. Not yet.

CHAPTER SEVEN

It was quiet in the office the next morning. With the bar was closed until midday, it gave Liam some time to get paperwork sorted, and his thoughts in check.

Seeing Angie last night had left him shaking. At first, he thought his own eyes were playing tricks on him. Angie couldn't be in his bar, looking that gorgeous, yet somehow so tortured. Those dull brown eyes gave away she was suffering. The fire inside her that once lit her alive had sizzled to a dull ember.

After her husband had thrown a punch at him, Jax suggested they replay the CCTV footage and turn it into police to press charges. Liam watched the footage, but not for the attempted assault Angie's husband tried to inflict on him.

He watched Angie who stood on the sidelines, clutching the arm of her friend as her husband lost control and tried to attack him. The CCTV showed Angie really had been in his bar.

Jax had insisted on turning the video in, but Liam refused. His care factor for Angie's husband was below zero, but he refused to take any risks in hurting Angie.

The fire she ignited in his belly when he saw her confused him. Even though they didn't know each other all that well, the time he'd spent with her over Christmas created a connection he'd never had with any other woman, even his ex-girlfriend.

Angie was unlike anyone he'd ever met. It was why his heart was shattered when he left Gumtree Plains without her. A woman like her deserved so much better than a cheating husband who couldn't see the amazing woman right in front of him.

'Hello?' A voice called out from the bar.

Liam lifted his head from the paperwork and checked his watch. The bar wasn't due to open for another two hours. Even so, the distraction was welcome and gave him a break from emails and crunching numbers.

Liam pushed himself off the chair and headed out to the bar. Before he stepped out of his office, he stopped and held his breath. What if it was Angie calling out to him? His hands began to tremble at the thought of being alone with her again.

When he stepped out of his office, his shoulders relaxed. Maybe it was a sign he wasn't ready to have a conversation with Angie.

'Catherine, hi. What're you doing here?'

Catherine stood half a metre away from the bar in a sleek black dress and tall pencil heels that accentuated her toned legs. Her brunette hair was pulled up into a high bun today, and those brown eyes batted behind large glasses.

He'd forgotten she wasn't wearing glasses last night when she came to the bar.

A black jacket hung over her arm, along with a black handbag, as she stood perfectly straight.

'Hi, Liam. I wanted to check in and see how everything was going with the new bar.'

Liam folded his arms. This was the most female attention he'd had in months, and if he was honest, he kind of liked it. 'That's certainly good customer service.'

'Well, I do try to go above and beyond for my clients. The best marketing is word of mouth. But I also wanted to check how you were after last night.'

'You mean after the attempted assault?' Liam unfolded his arms.

Catherine made him hyper aware of every move he made, like she was watching him intently with a critical eye.

Acting cool wasn't his strength. He reached under the counter and grabbed a tea towel to pretend he was wiping down the already spotless bench.

'Yes, that. I can't believe he took a swing at you. The guy's a nutcase and was totally out of line. I hope you're okay.'

'Did you see the size of him?' Liam said with a laugh. 'I'm fine,' he continued.

Catherine smiled, but didn't reply. Silence filled the air and he wished he'd turned on the music before he'd stepped out so there was something to fill the emptiness in their conversation.

'I might also have another agenda,' Catherine began as she stepped towards the bar. The harsh lights above them made her porcelain skin glow.

'I really enjoyed seeing you last night and wondered if you'd like to join me for dinner sometime.'

Liam almost tripped over his own feet as he pretended to clean the bench. He stopped and straightened his shirt, trying to maintain some dignity in front of this elegant woman.

'A date?' He scolded himself. The words sounded so immature.

Blush appeared on Catherine's cheeks and she glanced at the floor. When she looked back up at him, her eyes pierced straight through his heart. 'I guess you could call it that.'

Well, this is a first.

His immediate answer was no. The circumstances surrounding his and Angie's relationship was complicated. It had left him deflated and wondering where his life was going. But he'd also lost his chance with her.

He couldn't keep longing for someone who'd never love him back. And Catherine was beautiful. Smart. Genuine. A real catch. Whether or not he accepted Catherine's invitation didn't change Angie's marital status. She was never coming back to him. Holding out for a chance with her was futile.

'Okay,' Liam responded, surprised by his own confidence. 'I'd like that.'

'Excellent, I know the perfect place,' Catherine replied. 'How about you give me your number and I'll send you the deets.'

Liam pulled the smartphone from his pocket and handed it to her. After she entered the number into his phone, she held up the black jacket. 'Do you mind?'

'Not at all.' Liam stepped towards her and held the jacket up so she could insert her arms into either side.

Surely, this woman was playing a game. Standing next to her allowed her sweet perfume to fill his nostrils. It was different to Angie's perfume. It was more...mature. Where Angie's perfume was fun and flirty, Catherine's made a statement that she was here, and she was serious.

Once both her arms were in the jacket, she turned around and tugged it over her chest. 'You're a gentleman, Liam. I'm looking forward to dinner. I'll text you later.' Her eyes gazed over his body once, slowly, before turning on her black pencil heals and heading to the door.

'Look forward to it,' Liam replied, watching as her sensual hips swayed from side-to- side as she walked out of the bar.

CHAPTER EIGHT

It was lunchtime and Angie's feet ached from the constant switch between standing and sitting in court.

When she walked out of the Family Court, the cold wind whipped her in the face. It was a welcome distraction from the ache in her heart. The ache that had remained since she'd left Liam in Gumtree Plains to come back to Canberra with her adulterous husband.

When she got back to the office, a baby pink invitation was waiting in her inbox. 'Ugh,' she groaned as she opened the e-invite. It was for Jen's baby shower. Angie slumped back into the chair and gazed at the computer.

Of course, she was happy for Jen. But baby showers weren't really her thing. And if Liam was there, that would only complicate things.

She began formulating an email back, trying to make her rejection as polite and casual as possible.

Hi Jen, thanks for the invite. Sadly, I won't be able to make it as I have other plans that day. But please give me a forwarding address as I'd love to send a gift. Angie.

She clicked send.

A minute later, her smartphone buzzed on the desk.

That was fast.

'Jen, hi. How're you?'

'Well,' Jen began. 'I'm very pregnant and I'm not happy.'

'That'll pass,' Angie replied as she glanced at her watch. 'You'll be a mum soon enough. Not long to go now until you'll have bubs in your arms.'

'No, Angie. I'm not unhappy about being heavily pregnant and looking like the side of a house. I'm unhappy because you rejected my baby shower invitation.'

Angie's back stiffened and she sat up straight in the chair. 'Sorry, Jen. I've already got plans that day.'

'Like what, exactly?' Jen didn't beat around the bush and it caught Angie off guard. It was normally Angie who was straight to the point.

'Um,' Angie said without thinking, attempting to fill the air with words. *Any* words.

'To me, it sounds like a cop out. Does this have something to do with Liam?' Jen asked.

Angie paused before answering. 'Maybe.'

'You don't have to worry about him. I expect to see you there.'

'I really can't—'

'Do you want to piss off a pregnant woman? Because I might go into early labour if you do.'

'I guess not,' Angie replied.

'And I'd love it if you brought a plus one. Maybe a friend. It's a high tea so I doubt your husband will be interested.'

'You're probably right about that. I'll see you later.' Angie ended the call.

After placing the phone on the desk, she slid down the chair and lay back, resting her head on the soft leather. How did everything become so complicated?

When Jen had asked about a plus one, most people would instantly think of their significant other. Instead, Angie mentally cycled through the people she'd rather take. Michael was at the bottom of the list.

There was a knock at the door.

Angie pushed herself up in her seat and called out, 'Come in.'

Her secretary, Jessica, stood at the door in a long, cream boho dress with floppy sleeves and tan sandels. Curly chestnut hair flowed down her back and was pinned at the side.

When Angie had first interviewed her, she had reservations about Jessica's free-spiritedness. She wanted someone organised and focused, but it was a clear case of judging a book by its cover. Jessica was brilliant and the clients loved her.

'Your one p.m. has rescheduled.'

Angie resisted an eye roll. 'She's rescheduled three times now.'

Jessica's expression remained unchanged.

'Thanks, Jessica,' Angie corrected herself.

'That technically gives you just over an hour to head into the city and grab a present for your friend's baby shower.'

'What?' Angie asked.

'I have access to your emails, remember?'

'Oh, right,' Angie said as she glanced at her watch again. Jessica was efficient. *Too* efficient. 'I guess I'll be heading out to a baby shop then.'

'I'll grab your coat,' Jessica said with a grin.

* * *

Angie stood in the baby shop, surrounded by pregnant women and their partners, swanning through the aisles of polished laminate floor, pushing trolleys and picking up ridiculously expensive items from the pristine white shelves. Why did baby items cost the earth?

Angie leaned down to look at the price of a pram.

Bloody hell. I'd have to re-mortgage my apartment to shop here.

The music playing overhead was soft classical, and Angie wondered whether the calming environment unconsciously made people hand over their credit cards.

'Can I help you?' A woman asked, appearing at Angie's side.

Angie glanced over her shoulder at the young, smiling woman. Admittedly, everything that had been going on was starting to wear her down, and the woman's overly enthusiastic smile made her feel like she needed to fake one back.

'I'm just browsing.'

'For yourself?'

Angie's shoulders slumped. Having a baby with Michael was a terrible idea and would only end in heartache. But that didn't mean she didn't want one. Or two. Eventually.

'No,' she replied. 'It's for my friend's baby shower.'

'Wonderful. We have bibs and other toys that you could put into a nice little pack for the new mum. Or is there something you're looking for specifically?' The exaggerated grin remained on the young woman's face.

Where to start? The place was more like a warehouse than a boutique shop for babies. Sneakers would've been a more suitable footwear choice to get around this place.

Instead, Angie looked like an uptight corporate snob in a black suit and heels that were blistering the backs of her feet.

'What's the latest must-have for new mums?' If she was going to be forced to sit through Jen opening presents and her friends crooning over how cute they were, Angie was determined to get the best gift of all.

'I have the perfect thing. Follow me.' The young woman led Angie down an aisle of cots, prams and bouncers.

Angie's eyes bulged at the prices.

Two thousand dollars for a crib? It better be made of gold.

She kept a straight face as she walked along the laminate floors and realised babies were expensive. Damn expensive.

'Here we are.' The young woman picked up a box and thrust it towards Angie.

Angie examined the box. 'What is it?'

'It helps the mum and bub bond in the first few weeks to months by keeping skin-on-skin contact. It can cover their face in the sun and has support for mum's back. They've been super popular. It's the last one left.'

Angie turned the box over and looked at the price.

Holy hell.

'If you want something a bit cheaper, I'd suggest buying a basket and putting some creams and soaps in there. New mums love that. I certainly appreciated it when I had mine.' The smile remained.

'How many do you have?' Angie asked.

'Two little girls. They're my world.'

Angie forced a smile.

How cute. The nineteen-year old serving me has had more luck in the love department than me.

'Let's go with this,' Angie said as she held up the box.

'Great, I'll put it through the checkout for you,' the woman said as she walked back to the counter.

Angie pulled out the platinum gold credit card and swiped it across the card machine.

'Sorry, the payment was declined,' the young woman said as she ripped off the receipt.

'There must be something wrong with the machine,' Angie replied. 'I'll try it again,' she said as she swiped the card once more.

A moment later, the woman said, 'Sorry, it's declined again. Do you have another card?' The woman's enthusiastic smile turned into a grimace.

It was the debit card she shared with Michael. The account always had money it. With a large line of pregnant couples waiting to be served, she wasn't taking another chance. She pulled her personal debit card from her wallet and swiped it.

'Approved,' the young woman said. The overzealous smile returned to her face. 'I'm sure your friend will love the gift. Bye now,' she said as she slipped the receipt into the bag and handed it over to Angie.

'Thanks,' Angie said with a nod as she exited the store to return to work, still perplexed over why the card had declined in the first place.

CHAPTER NINE

Wednesday night rolled around faster than Liam expected. He didn't think Catherine would follow through on her promise of calling him, but she proved to be a woman of her word.

Despite accepting the invitation, Liam still wasn't sure he was ready for a date. He stood by the bar drinking a glass of soft drink when a hand slipped over his lower back.

The touch set his skin on fire and ignited a memory of the night he'd spent with Angie at Christmas in Gumtree Plains. The night her hands pulled him inside her, wanting, yearning for every inch of him.

That was the night Liam dreamed about. The memory he wanted so bad to forget.

'It's good to see you, Liam,' the woman said as she leaned in and planted a kiss on his cheek.

The touch of her lips left a tingle on his skin. The hand she'd placed on his back didn't move, remaining just above his belt.

He cleared his throat. 'G'day, Catherine.'

'Ready to go?'

Liam nodded. 'Sure am.' He waved over the bar to let Jax know he was leaving. 'See ya, mate. Have a good time,' Jax called out.

'I promise to bring him back in one piece,' Catherine replied with a wink.

* * *

The restaurant was fancy. Too fancy. Being in the service industry, Liam knew they were only doing their jobs, but he hated people making a fuss over him.

'Can I take your coat, sir?' the waiter asked.

'It's fine,' Liam replied. He didn't need anyone taking his coat, especially a kid fresh out of high school.

'Thank you,' Catherine said as she slipped out of her long, black coat and revealed a figure-hugging navy-blue dress. Liam gulped. It'd been months since he'd been physical with a woman.

Watching Catherine take her seat in that dress sent his heart racing. The waiter continued fussing over them and pulled out his chair, tucking him in a little too close to the table.

'Thank you, I'll take it from here,' Liam stated firmly.

'This is my favourite restaurant. What do you think?' Catherine asked as she peered up at him from behind the sleek menu.

Liam glanced around the joint. The lights were dim, making it the ideal spot for a romantic evening, or couples who wanted to be hidden from plain sight. The tables were far enough away that they could have a private conversation, and the mellow music created a smooth atmosphere.

Yet Liam couldn't relax. He'd read about this place. It was a hatted restaurant, and that meant something to restaurant-goers. Liam was a simple country boy. He didn't know anything about fancy food and wine.

When he'd first heard the term, he thought a hatted restaurant was where you wore a hat while eating the food.

'My name's Josh and I'll be your waiter tonight. Have you had a chance to look at the drinks menu?'

'Yes,' Catherine replied. 'Can I please have a glass of the house red?'

'Of course, madam. And for you, sir?'

The list of red wines on the menu ran over three pages. This wine went with that meal and so on.

Liam drank beer, almost exclusively, and only the occasional white wine. Never red. Liam glanced up at the waiter and handed back the menu. 'I'll take a beer, thanks.'

Catherine's eyebrows shot up and she stared at him across the table.

'Are you sure you don't want a red wine? They source the best wines from around the country here.'

'I'm fine with a beer.'

'We only have two beers available, sir. Are you sure you wouldn't prefer a red wine?'

'Whatever beer you have on tap is fine,' Liam said, standing his ground.

Catherine cleared her throat before whispering, 'They don't do tap. They only have bottles.'

Bloody hell.

'Okay then, whatever you have in a *bottle* is fine,' he replied, glancing up at the waiter and handing him the drinks menu.

'One beer coming up and one of our finest reds,' he said as he noted the order and headed to the kitchen.

'Not a red wine drinker?'

'Not a big drinker,' Liam admitted. 'Don't have the taste buds for red wine.'

'It's an acquired taste,' Catherine replied as she tossed the hair off her shoulder.

Liam noted his knees, bouncing up and down frantically. What was happening? Catherine was a beautiful woman. Smart. Enchanting. Normally he'd take this as a challenge. There was nothing wrong with an intellectual conversation. But being with this woman made him sweat.

'Here you are, madam,' the waiter said as he placed the large glass of red wine on the table.

'Thank you,' she said as she lifted the glass, swirled the wine and smelled it before taking a sip.

'So, Liam. You're from the country. What part?'

'Gumtree Plains. It's in the Snowy Mountains. A beautiful spot. My folks own a brumby-spotting business.'

'I see,' Catherine replied with a raised brow.

'What about you? Where're you from?'

Catherine ran her long fingers through her dark hair, never taking her eyes off Liam.

'I was born in Canberra, grew up in Sydney. Even though I live in Canberra now, I can never forget my one true love, the Northern Beaches. There's something about that place that brings me to life. I love nightclubs, the beach and eating out. And wineries. I can't say no to a good wine...'

'That's—'

'And my parents own a lovely house by the water. I try to get there as often as I can.'

'Sounds like you—'

'It really is a shame I don't get there more often, but work is just so demanding.'

The talking continued.

Liam couldn't get a word in. Bouts of verbal diarrhea kept blurting from Catherine's mouth. She didn't even come up for air, and he wondered whether she'd notice if he went to the bathroom and didn't come back.

'Are we ready to order now?'

About bloody time.

'Yes,' Liam announced, a little too enthusiastically. 'I'll take the, uh, the steak and mashed potato.'

'Wonderful choice. The steak *et purée de pommes de terre* is fabulous,' the waiter said.

'I don't doubt that,' Liam replied. He hated when people referred to food in French. To Liam, it was plain old steak and mashed potatoes.

They both gave their menus to the waiter.

'Anyway, as I was saying,' Catherine continued.

Liam didn't want to appear rude, so he stared at the cowlick in her hair at the front of her forehead. At least that way it looked like he was paying attention. 'Liam?'

The voice was familiar.

'What a pleasant surprise.' The tone of Catherine's voice implied she *wasn't* pleasantly surprised. Regardless, she stood up and hugged the woman who was significantly shorter than her.

The black floral jumpsuit didn't do her justice. And Liam knew exactly what was hiding under the material.

'Angie.' Liam sat up straight in the uncomfortable metal seat.

'Hello, Liam.'

Her blonde hair sat past her shoulders in soft curls, emphasising the roundness of her face.

'Hi, Liam. I'm Lizzie, Angie's friend.' Lizzie offered her hand to him.

Liam stood to his feet and shook her hand. 'Of course, I remember you, Lizzie. Good to see you again. You two here for dinner?'

'Yeah, it's a bit of a Wednesday night ritual. We normally get takeaway, but thought we should do something special after Angie's win.'

'Angie's win?' Liam was interested.

Who was he kidding? Anything to do with Angie interested him.

'Oh, you didn't hear?' Lizzie continued. Her eyes shifted quickly to Angie, then back to Liam. 'Angie just won an award for up-and-coming young lawyer of the year. You better watch out. She's going to make partner soon.' Lizzie grinned and gave Angie a soft nudge in the arm.

'We'll see,' Angie replied, not so enthusiastically. Angie's cheeks turned a pale shade of pink and she wouldn't let her eyes meet Liam's.

All he wanted was to stare into those eyes, to search for answers as to why she never contacted him. Even after she'd ripped his heart out of his chest while it was still beating, he still wanted to embrace her in his arms.

'It was lovely seeing you,' Catherine said, interrupting his thoughts. 'Enjoy your dinner.'

CHAPTER TEN

Angie's hands shook as she grabbed the corner of the table, making the glasses of water rock like there was an impending earthquake.

'You okay?' Lizzie asked, as she gave her jacket to the waiter.

Angie shook her head, unable to speak.

Why did they have to come to this place tonight? Why did Liam have to be at the exact place at the same time with *her*?

'What do you think they're doing here together?' Angie asked.

'It's pretty obvious they're on a date,' Lizzie replied.

The bile rose in Angie's throat. She had no reason to be jealous or upset. She was married. She *chose* to stay with her husband.

But every day was a struggle. Living with a man who she resented couldn't go on for much longer. Liam was what she craved. To wake up next to him. To share life with him. Sadly, that chance was over now. He'd moved on with someone she despised.

'We're here to celebrate. Let's not dwell on what stuck-up Catherine's doing,' Lizzie said as she opened the menu.

Angie didn't want to hear Lizzie say her name. Catherine was Angie's arch enemy. They'd spent years at law school competing to get the highest grades, the best internships, the most prestigious job.

'How can I just sit here knowing she's probably telling Liam the same lies she spread about me at uni?'

Lizzie looked up from the menu. 'Everyone who knows you knows you didn't sleep with your professor.'

'You and I know it's not true, but Liam doesn't. I've been trying to escape that rumour for years,' Angie said as she glared in Catherine's direction.

Lizzie waved her hand in the air to get Angie's attention. 'Stop.

Leave them be. You can't control what she says, but you and I both know she's a wacko,' Lizzie said as she re-opened the menu.

When Angie looked back on it now, she realised how petty it was. How immature she'd been to think the only thing that mattered in the world was superb grades.

University flew by in a blur and when she graduated, Angie couldn't believe she'd missed the most important part—the experience.

'You're right. Let's not dwell on that.' Angie reached into the middle of the table to grab the menu when her smartphone sounded with a message. She picked it up and looked at the screen. When she saw the name, her stomach backflipped.

'I have to go outside for a second.'

'Do you want me to order for you?' Lizzie asked.

'I'll take whatever you're having.' As Angie pushed herself off her chair, the waiter appeared.

'Is everything okay, madam?'

'Yes, everything's fine. I need to go outside for a moment,' she said as her heart pounded.

'Would you like your coat?'

'It's fi—' before she could finish the sentence, the waiter rushed over to the coat rack. He came back within a minute and held it out for her to put her arms in.

This was the kind of place her parents loved, but the constant fussing over the customers made her uncomfortable.

'Thank you,' she said as she adjusted the coat and pushed the buttons through the holes. When she opened the door of the restaurant, the chill of the autumn air hit her face and cooled her burning cheeks.

She tugged the jacket over her chest to keep the chill from prickling her skin. She poked her head around the corner and spotted *him* leaning against the brick wall.

The sight of him constricted her lungs.

How could he look even better than when she last saw him? It was like there was a rope tied between them, pulling her closer towards him.

There was no point resisting. It only made the urge stronger.

As she neared him, he pushed himself off the wall.

'Angie,' he breathed as he wrapped his arms around her shoulders.

There was no resisting his touch. The touch she'd yearned to feel for months. Angie leaned into the hug, releasing the breath she'd been holding, letting her body relax against his warm, strong embrace.

Her stomach tightened as the place between her thighs began to pulse.

'I missed you,' he said when he stepped away from the wall. He only looked into her eyes for a moment before he grabbed her by the waist and pulled her body into his.

Their lips met and he kissed her, the same way he'd kissed her on Christmas day. There was an urgency to his kiss. A wanting that couldn't be ignored. Angie didn't resist. Didn't *want* to resist. She couldn't. There was something about Liam that made her completely lose her composure.

She wrapped her arms around his broad shoulders and squeezed them. The muscles in his back tensed under her palms. It made the place between her legs pulse harder.

Liam turned her in a circle and pressed her back against the brick wall as he kissed her lips, her neck, under the cold chill of the autumn evening.

Holy shit.

His hands travelled under her shirt towards her breasts. The touch of his skin sent waves of electricity through her entire body.

'Liam,' she breathed, unable to stop the moan escaping her lips.

'Angie?'

The voice calling her name sounded distant and unreal. She ignored it and let Liam kiss her neck. Let the touch of his lips take her away from her sad reality.

'Angie!'

A hand tugged at her jacket and she jumped to face the intruder.

'What the fuck are you two doing?' Lizzie cursed. Her gaze shifted between them both, demanding an answer.

It made Angie acutely aware she'd been caught red-handed making out with a man who *wasn't* her husband.

'I...ah.' There were no words to explain what she was doing. Being with Liam made her lose all sense of time.

'Catherine's looking for you, Liam.' Lizzie snapped. Then she turned her attention to Angie. 'And you're lucky I found you out here instead of Catherine. I don't want to imagine what kind of a scene she would've caused. She almost destroyed your reputation last time.'

Lizzie shot one more glare at them before grabbing Angie's hand and pulling her back towards the restaurant.

Angie looked back at Liam as Lizzie pulled her away from him. This was the part she hated. The part that split her heart in two as the distance between them grew.

Liam's eyes stared at the ground. Of course he couldn't watch her walk away. Not again. Her heart urged her to break free from Lizzie's grip and grab Liam's hand. To run away with him, back to Gumtree Plains where they could be together.

'What were you thinking? Are you on drugs?' Lizzie demanded in a whisper as they walked back into the restaurant.

'I wasn't thinking. I don't think when I'm around him,' Angie replied as her eyes flitted around the restaurant, still on a high from what happened outside.

'Do you know how lucky you are that I caught you and not Catherine? She would've ripped your head off.'

'She doesn't even know him!' Angie cried as she turned towards Lizzie.

The entire restaurant stopped talking and looked in her direction. Angie's back stiffened and she swallowed under the unexpected attention.

Lizzie's eyes widened. Angie's hands began to tremble from the confrontation. A stand-off with Catherine was the last thing she needed right now, but what was Liam even doing with her? Did she have a right to know? She'd given him no closure when she left Gumtree Plains with Michael.

Liam owed her nothing and had every right to move on. That didn't mean her heart wasn't torn apart knowing he was moving on with someone else. Her enemy, nonetheless.

'Would you keep it down,' Lizzie ordered. For once, it was Lizzie speaking sense and being the mature one in their friendship.

The door of the restaurant opened and Liam walked inside. His shirt was now straight and he didn't give away any indication they'd been caught red-handed making out against the brick wall of a five-star restaurant. He strolled over to the table where Catherine was sitting.

Catherine didn't even look at him. She stared in Angie's direction with a stiff jaw and narrow eyes.

Angie couldn't pull her eyes away from him. Liam was the person she longed for every night when she went to bed. The man she craved when she woke.

When loneliness struck her heart, his face was the first to appear in her mind. Yet she could never have him. Not after everything that had happened. Not when she was married to someone else.

'I'm sorry, Lizzie. I have to go.'

'Angie,' Lizzie replied.

Angie didn't listen. She grabbed her handbag from the coat rack and ran out the door of the restaurant.

CHAPTER ELEVEN

'She's always been *so* overdramatic,' Catherine purred as she swirled the glass of red wine in her hand. She smelled the wine, before sipping from the glass with closed eyes.

There was a bitterness to Catherine's tone, like she had a personal vendetta against Angie.

'I see she's not your favourite person?' Liam queried as he sliced the thin piece of beef on his plate.

It was unbelievable the restaurant was charging sixty bucks for this tiny plate of mashed potato puree, a thin piece of beef and three leaves on the side.

You can hardly call two leaves a salad.

'I don't hate anyone, but if I did, it would be her,' Catherine spat.

She placed the glass next to her plate. It was her fourth wine of the night. The professional Catherine Liam had met a week earlier was strikingly different to the woman sitting in front of him now.

Some of her mascara had smudged, and her cheeks had flushed pink from the hot air circulating in the restaurant. It wasn't as if the wine made her happy either.

'You hate Angie?'

Her eyes flickered up from her plate. 'I didn't say that.'

The comment forced heat to rise in Liam's cheeks. He couldn't imagine anyone hating Angie. Sweet, kind Angie. The light in a very dark world. The only woman who'd made him love and hurt at the same time.

'What's your history with Angie?' Liam asked, finally interested in something Catherine had to say.

'She's competitive and will do anything to win. I'm not saying I'm

Mother Teresa, but at least I didn't cheat.'

'Cheat?'

Catherine picked up the glass of wine again and swirled it in her hand. 'Let's just say she can be very charming with men when she wants to get ahead.'

Liam stared at Catherine. 'Are you saying Angie slept with someone to get ahead?'

Catherine waved her hand in the air. 'Pretend I never said anything. All I know is that woman should never have been admitted to practice law in the first place.'

Liam placed the cutlery beside his plate. Catherine was accusing Angie of cheating and sleeping her way to the top? In any circumstance, this wasn't good. But was there any truth to what she'd said?

'She doesn't seem like the type of person who'd do something like that. Are you sure?' Liam questioned.

Catherine swirled the wine glass in her hand. 'One hundred percent.'

* * *

'Liam, thank you for a wonderful night,' Catherine said as they strolled through the city, back to *Cowboys*.

Catherine stopped drinking after the fourth glass and once she'd sobered up, she seemed to return to her normal, carefree self.

'Would you like to come in for a coffee?' he asked as they stood outside the staircase of the bar.

The soft guitar strums filtered out into the street, bringing back the memory of being home on the farm with hi family.

'I really shouldn't. I have a big day at work tomorrow.'

Liam wasn't sure about where their friendship would go, and he wasn't sure whether he was romantically interested in Catherine. Her beauty and intelligence may have been too much for him.

'Well, thank you for a fun night.' As he was about to step into *Cowboys*, Catherine grabbed his hand, pulling him towards her, and kissed him on the lips.

Liam's eyes burst open as their mouths moved together. The touch of her warm tongue on his overwhelmed his senses. The red wine was too strong, and he tried to pull away.

But she kept a tight grip on him and moved her hands around his waist so he couldn't escape.

Catherine continued kissing him, moaning as her mouth moved against his rigid lips. It wasn't right. In fact, the kiss made him feel nothing.

His mind transported him back to the moment he and Angie shared at Gumtree Lakehouse. Their giggling. Their skin touching. Their bodies completely entwined. Those memories made Liam close his eyes, wishing he could go back to that place. Wishing he was kissing Angie instead of Catherine.

After a moment, Catherine pulled away and smiled. 'You were a bit limp to start with, but you're a good kisser,' she said with a grin.

Liam cleared his throat. Admitting to her he was thinking of Angie would never escape his lips. He'd take that secret to the grave.

'Well, I'd best be off, cowboy. I'd love to see you again.'

Liam didn't know how to respond, so he nodded.

Catherine blew him a kiss as she headed to her car parked by the kerb. Liam watched her drive off, just to make sure she was safe, then headed upstairs to *Cowboys*.

'Back so soon, mate? I thought you were going to be out for the whole night, if you know what I mean.' Jax winked as he poured a drink for a customer. Jax had been pushing him to date, play the field to get over Angie.

Liam didn't want a bar of it. In his experience, sleeping with women to get over a broken heart was a terrible idea and only fraught with more heartache.

'Nothing to see here, mate.'

'Your sister in-law called,' Jax said as Liam headed out to the office to grab his uniform.

'Jen?'

'Yeah. Something about a baby shower. You'd better call her back. She said she'd have it in for me if you didn't.'

'I'll call her now. Give me five.' Liam punched the number into the phone and sat down behind his desk.

'Liam, where've you been?' Jen demanded when she answered the phone.

'Hello to you too. How did you know it was me?'

'Who else calls this late? Besides, I told your buddy he'd be in big trouble if you didn't call me back tonight.'

Liam chuckled to himself. 'Alright, alright. What's wrong?'

'My baby shower's on Saturday and I expect you there. So does Harry.'

'My brother's going to your baby shower? I thought baby showers were just an excuse for women to eat cupcakes and go gaga when the mother-to-be opens presents.'

'Harry contributed fifty percent to this pregnancy, so he doesn't have a choice. And as the uncle of my unborn child, neither do you. Besides, who doesn't like cupcakes? They're delicious.' Jen was getting bossier by the second.

'Whatever you say, Jen.'

'And you have to bring a plus one.'

'What if I don't have a plus one to bring?' The request seemed strange. Jen knew he didn't have a girlfriend.

'Well you'd better find one. And it has to be a woman.'

'A woman? What's with all these demands?' Liam sat up in the chair and pressed his elbows against the desk.

'Because I have a plan.'

'A plan for what?' His sister-in-law was starting to sound crazy.

Maybe it was baby brain.

'Liam, I don't care who she is, just bring a female date, okay? I'll email you the details in the morning.'

'Alright,' Liam conceded. There was no arguing with the heavily pregnant Jen. She was a force to be reckoned with.

When he hung up the phone, he stared at the screen of his smartphone. Where could his relationship with Catherine possibly go? He couldn't ask Angie to go with him, even if he wanted to. Dating a married woman was off the table in his books. But he wasn't going to defy his sister in-law. It was her baby shower and if she wanted something, he'd do everything in his power to satisfy her request.

He opened a new text and started typing.

Are you up for a baby shower on the weekend?

He put the phone on the desk and stood up to change his shirt. Before he left the office, it buzzed on the desk.

I thought you'd never ask. Count me in.

CHAPTER TWELVE

'I don't like this one bit,' Michael complained from the other side of the kitchen on Saturday morning.

Angie rubbed her temples with her index fingers. She'd had a headache for a few days now. The fights with Michael seemed to trigger them. He was picking fights over anything these days. Her work hours. The groceries she bought. He even started a fight over turning up the television too loud.

Having to constantly defend herself was draining her energy completely. There was no fight left in her. This marriage wasn't worth it.

'Michael, your behaviour towards me is concerning,' Angie replied as she lathered a piece of multigrain toast with strawberry jam.

'*My* behaviour is concerning?' he questioned. 'What are you, a psychiatrist now?'

Angie dropped the butter knife and slammed her hands on the bench. 'No, Michael, I'm not a psychiatrist. I'm a fucking divorce lawyer. I see this all the time. Partners who start out making nasty comments about their spouses. Trying to control their finances. Telling them they can't go out with their friends. Keeping them from doing the things they want to do. Trying to stop them from being independent!'

Michael's jaw dropped. 'You're painting me with the same brush of a man who abuses his wife?'

'Oh, please. Don't pretend you're so shocked,' she bit back as she slammed the door of the fridge after putting away the jam. 'You've been abusive to me in the past. Not just verbally, but physically too.'

'Like when?' he demanded, his voice rising higher. 'When have I ever been physical with you?' he mocked. 'I've given you everything.

Everything! And then you accuse me of being a wife beater?'

'The night I won my award. Remember? When you grabbed my hand and wouldn't let go. That's how it starts out. How do I know you won't lose your shit completely one day and put me in hospital?'

His mouth dropped open. 'You…you're delusional, Angie. You're fucking delusional,' he repeated as he threw his hands in the air. 'You know what? I'm sick of this. I'm going out. And don't worry about telling me where you're going. It's not like I give a shit about who you hang out with.'

Five minutes later, after changing into jeans and a white t-shirt, Michael left the apartment.

When the door slammed shut behind him, Angie burst into tears. The fight had lasted thirty minutes. The constant nagging, surveillance of her activities and accusations had finally worn her down. She was close to breaking point.

What she really wanted to do was to sit on the couch and cry. She didn't want to go to Jen's baby shower, not after what had just happened.

Her marriage was like an out of control train heading full speed into the fiery depths of hell. And Liam had moved on. Maybe there was no hope for her to be happy. Maybe working so hard for her career had finally come at a price.

One bite of the toast and she was full. Angie hadn't been eating much, and when she was stressed, it erased her appetite completely.

She glanced up at the kitchen clock and realised she only had fifteen minutes to get ready.

Despite wishing she didn't have to go, she owed it to Jen to show up. And who knew. Maybe she'd enjoy herself without Michael watching her every move.

* * *

Angie stood at the steps of the hotel with the wrapped present in her arms.

A big, yellow bow sat atop the box and she hated that everyone coming in and out of the hotel was staring.

The dress code was strictly floral. Angie's cupboard consisted of black and navy business suits. The dress was an impulse buy, and she was regretting how bright it was against the equally garish wrapping of the present.

'You ready?'

Angie looked over her shoulder at Lizzie, who resembled a housewife in a pink floral dress and black heels. The look suited her. No one would ever guess they dressed as corporate business women during the week.

'Come on then,' Lizzie urged as she climbed the first few steps of the hotel.

'Wait,' Angie called out. She clung to the box for security.

'What's wrong?' Lizzie asked.

'What if Liam's in there?'

Lizzie looked around at the other women walking into the establishment, all wearing floral dresses and carrying gifts.

'Angie, the dress code is old lady floral and we're attending a high tea at the fanciest hotel in town. I doubt men are invited to this event. In fact, I guarantee most wouldn't want to be seen dead here.'

Lizzie's words put Angie slightly at ease. She didn't want any slip-ups. Liam wasn't hers anymore. Letting him go was for the best.

Inside, the hotel staff had set up a high tea full of sugary goodness. Cupcakes, brownies, fudge, caramel slice, cakes, fruit platters and punch were placed across the long table on a white tablecloth.

There was enough food to feed a small nation. It was a standing affair to encourage the attendees to mingle. Angie searched the crowd for a familiar face. Then she saw Harry.

'I thought you said there'd be no men?' she whispered to Lizzie.

Lizzie looked across at Angie. 'Jen's your friend, not mine. Besides, I think that's the husband, isn't it? Makes sense that he's here.'

It was Harry, Liam's brother. The sight of him made Angie's stomach backflip. The brothers were so different in personality, but looked so similar. He was wearing a Hawaiian shirt, which fit the floral theme perfectly, but he looked flustered. Jen must've been bossing him around.

'Angie, you made it,' Jen announced when she spotted her from across the room. Jen waddled over, her large belly protruding in front.

She opened her arms and embraced Angie in a hug. It was hard to embrace her back when she was so far along in her pregnancy.

'You look like you're close to popping now,' Angie said.

'Due in three weeks,' Jen replied. She stared into Angie's eyes and smiled. 'How have you been, lovely?'

'Good,' Angie said with a forced smile.

'Come on. I know you better than that. How are you, really?'

It was a hard question to answer. No one had asked how she was. Instead of letting the feelings get to her, she pushed them deep down inside so she didn't have to deal with them. 'Honestly, Jen? Not great.'

'Husband troubles?'

Angie nodded. 'We had another fight this morning. He didn't want me to come today.'

Jen leaned in for another hug and whispered in her ear, 'I'm sorry you're going through this. I want you to enjoy the day, but I have to tell you something. Liam still loves you. You still have a chance.'

Angie froze.

Jen pulled away and rubbed her hands down Angie's arms. 'Trust me.' Then Jen walked away to greet some more guests.

'Angie?'

Angie turned to face Lizzie. 'Yeah?'

'You know how I said there'd probably be no men. Well, turns out I was wrong.' Lizzie tilted her head to the entrance.

Angie's eyes locked with his and she couldn't tear them away. But he was with someone else. Liam was with *her*.

CHAPTER THIRTEEN

This can't be happening. Again.

Liam was standing at the entrance of the hotel and in the distance was the woman of his dreams. The woman he could never have.

He could've asked himself the question why she was there, but that was redundant. Jen never let anything slip regarding her friendship with Angie.

The thought of Angie attending today hadn't even crossed his mind. But seeing her made him realise something. Jen wasn't being cryptic. She wanted him to bring a date to to the baby shower to make Angie jealous.

He hated when Jen stuck her nose where it didn't belong. Now there was the potential for a serious scene to break out.

Catherine stepped beside him and huffed. 'Why is that bloody woman everywhere I go?' she muttered under her breath.

He didn't dare admit to Catherine it was because he and Angie shared a past.

'Angie's friends with my sister in-law.'

'How do they even know each other?' she asked. 'I thought your family lived in the sticks.'

'Gumtree Plains,' Liam corrected.

'Whatever,' Catherine said as she waved her hand in the air. 'Somewhere out in the middle of nowhere. I'm going to put an end to this.'

'An end to what?'

'Our feud.' She walked towards Angie.

Liam stepped in front of her and put his arms out. 'What're you doing?' she asked as she stared him up and down.

'Stopping you from causing a scene,' he whispered, trying to remain calm as his eyes shifted around the room.

'A scene?'

'Yes. This is my sister-in-law's baby shower. Don't bring your personal vendetta's in here today.'

'No one is causing a scene,' Catherine replied, trying to get past him.

'Catherine, come on,' Liam said as he reached out and touched her shoulder.

'No,' Catherine replied, shrugging his hand away.

He had no other option except to physically restrain her, but that wasn't an option in this venue. He'd be thrown out by security.

Catherine approached Angie and Liam followed close behind.

'I want to know something, Angie. How did you manage to get the top of Mr Broderick's class?'

Angie turned around and was holding a champagne glass. 'You again?' Angie's eyes narrowed when she spotted Catherine. 'When will you stop trying to drag my name through the mud?'

'Not until you admit what you did.'

'Seriously? You're still stuck on a rumour you started six years ago that never happened? Move on. It's pathetic. I'm sure everyone here would like you to calm down and enjoy this lovely high tea to celebrate Jen and Harry's baby.'

Angie turned to leave when Catherine grabbed her arm, stopping her exit.

Angie looked down at Catherine's hand. 'Let go of my arm,' Angie threatened. 'This won't end well for you if you don't.'

'If I don't? You should never have been admitted to practice. You're a cheater, in more ways than one!'

The guests at the baby shower paused and stared in Angie and Catherine's direction. Liam swallowed as he watched the scene unfold, not sure how to intervene.

The guests stared at the two women, holding champagne flutes of punch and nibbling on the spread of sugary food.

That's all Liam wanted to do right now. Enjoy a glass of punch and catch up with his brother. Instead, he was stuck in the middle of some argument between his date and the woman he loved.

'Keep your voice down,' Angie demanded. 'What're you trying to prove by doing this? That I slept with a professor six years ago? I don't owe you anything, especially an explanation. But for the record, I'd *never* sleep with a professor for a good grade. I won the highest grade in the class because I worked my arse off to get there.'

'You never should've won that award last week. You're not as competent as everyone thinks you are. That award belonged to *me*,' Catherine hissed.

Oh dear.

That's what this was about. Catherine was jealous of Angie and couldn't stand her success.

'Catherine, I didn't ask to win that award,' Angie replied whole still holding the glass of wine.

'Maybe not, but I bet you slept with the partners to get their vote. You know how these things work. Sleep your way to the top and get the career you want. You've gotten pretty good at that over the years, haven't you?'

'Stop it!' Lizzie's voice echoed throughout the hotel.

Silence followed.

Liam wasn't expecting that tone to come out of Lizzie's mouth.

'Elizabeth, stay out of this. It has nothing to do with you,' Catherine retorted.

'Actually, Catherine, it has everything to do with me,' Lizzie replied in a mocking tone.

'Stop defaming Angie in front of everyone here. If you want to fight this in court, keep running off your mouth. But if you say one more false statement about her, I'll be filing a case against you in court next week on Angie's behalf. I dare you to say one more thing. Do it,' she dared.

Catherine opened her mouth to say something, but the words never came out.

'Fine. Enjoy your baby shower.' Catherine turned on her heels and headed for the door. Before she left opened, she turned back and called out to Liam. 'Are you coming?'

Liam stared at her over his shoulder. She was crazy if she thought he'd go with her after the scene she'd just caused.

'Go on without me.'

'What?' She glared at him with narrowed eyes.

He may have been a simple country boy, but he was no pushover.

'I've seen enough here, Catherine. Goodbye and all the best.'

'Oh, and one more thing, Catherine,' Lizzie announced as she walked up behind Liam. She linked her arm with his and smiled. 'Liam's with us.'

* * *

'I told you to bring a date, not a recent escapee from the local psych ward,' Jen whispered as she sipped non-alcoholic punch from a champagne flute. They were standing back from the table, taking time out from a hectic start to the baby shower.

'Very funny,' Liam replied with an eye roll. 'Though I am sorry for the scene she caused. I guess she has a lot of insecurities.'

'No need to apologise. If anything, it brought this party to life. No one likes baby showers anyway,' Jen replied as she grabbed a cupcake from the table.

'I'm glad you finally understand that,' Liam teased.

'Besides, I don't blame Catherine for acting the way she did. I mean, I'd probably do the same thing too.'

Liam crossed his arms. 'What's that supposed to mean?'

'Everyone knows you're in love with Angie. It's clear to everyone else except you two oblivious idiots.'

Liam unfolded his arms and sighed. Even the mention of her name made his heart ache. 'It doesn't matter because she's married.'

'Her husband's a jerk. And she doesn't want to be with him.'

'She told you that?'

Jen tilted her head and looked across at Liam. 'She didn't have to.'

Liam allowed himself to process the information as they watched the guests mingle and chat. 'What're you saying, Jen? I should declare my love to her?'

Jen gave her empty champagne flute to a passing waiter. 'I'm saying if you don't tell her how you feel, you'll regret it for the rest of your life. I know she feels the same, even if she won't admit it.'

At that moment, Angie walked past them to grab a glass of punch.

'Hey, Angie. Can I borrow you for a sec?'

Angie turned around. The floral dress flowed off her hips and showed off more cleavage than usual.

'Liam has something to tell you.'

'Wait, what?' Liam glared at Jen as she left him and stepped back into the crowd of guests.

Angie smiled in his direction.

'Hi.'

'Hi,' she replied.

'Perhaps we should find a spot that's a little more private?'

She nodded. 'Sure. Let's go out to the courtyard.'

* * *

Liam and Angie sat on a bench in the courtyard at the back of the hotel. It overlooked a lush, freshly mown lawn, surrounded by a manicured garden. Birds chirped in the aviary and the air was fresh, yet comfortable for an autumn day.

'Your birthday must be coming up soon.'

'Tomorrow, actually,' she replied.

'Wow. We've known each other a year already? Time really does fly,' Liam said as he linked his fingers together in his lap.

Angie nodded and stared into the distance.

'Doing anything special?'

Angie shrugged. 'You know I hate birthdays. I'd rather not make a fuss and let it pass without noticing.'

'Come on,' Liam replied. 'Last year's birthday was pretty good, if I remember correctly.'

A shade of pink rose to her cheeks, and she tried to hide behind the champagne flute. 'So, Liam. What did you want to talk about?'

There was the Angie he knew and loved. Never one to beat around the bush. He sighed and took a moment to bask in the warm sun.

'This won't be easy to say, so I'm just going to say it.' He paused for a moment. 'It's been hell without you. The time we spent together at Christmas was the best and worst time of my life. Coming back to Canberra without you was like losing someone I've loved my whole life. I'm still not over you, and don't know if I ever will be.'

Angie didn't move or say anything. Instead, she took another sip of punch.

'Are you going to say anything?' he asked.

Her gaze was fixed in the distance at the perfect garden in front of them. The aviary, a few metres away, housed all types of birds. They chirped and boasted a symphony of colours from the rainbow. When she looked back at him, a tear streamed down her cheek.

'I'm not over you either,' she admitted.

While Liam was relieved to hear it, the sentence sounded unfinished. 'But...'

'I'm married to someone else.'

The comment kicked him in the guts. 'How's that working out for you?' The tone in his voice was more bitter than he intended.

'Terribly. He's a prick and I resent him more and more every day. He makes me feel awful about myself.'

'So why don't you leave him then?' Liam genuinely wanted to understand why she chose to stay with someone she couldn't stand.

'I'm trying.'

'What's stopping you?'

Angie sighed and stared at the glass in her hand. 'Loyalty.'

'Do you love him?' Liam's question must've hit a nerve. Angie pinched her eyes together and wiped the tears away with the back of her hand.

'No, I don't.'

'So, come home with me, right now.'

'It's not that easy, Liam. I can't just walk out of my marriage.'

Liam was sick of this. He was sick of coming second to Michael when all the guy had done was treat Angie like dirt. She deserved better, but so did Liam.

Liam pressed his fingers against his temples. 'Angie, I can't do this with you anymore. I can't keep loving you, wishing for you to come back to me. I can't keep waiting and hoping you'll call to tell me you're ready. So, this is my ultimatum,' Liam announced as he stood to his feet.

Angie looked up at him from the bench. Her eyes squinted under the bright sun.

'It's him or it's me. Who do you choose?'

Angie's glassy eyes stared up at him. She said nothing.

'I'm not kidding. You can't expect me to wait around for you forever. It's not fair for me to keep hoping for a relationship that may never happen.'

Angie broke eye contact and sniffled as another tear fell.

'Angie, I need to know now.'

Her eyes stuck like glue to the freshly mown grass.

A minute passed.

No words.

'That's it? You have nothing left to say to me? After everything we've been through?

Silence.

It was too much. His heart cracked open again and threatened to reveal itself to the world.

'Angie, if I walk out of this hotel, there's no coming back. I'm moving on, for good this time. With or without you.'

Angie froze. No words. No actions. Nothing.

He had his answer. Without waiting a second longer, Liam walked out of the courtyard and headed for the hotel exit.

CHAPTER FOURTEEN

The tears rolled freely down Angie's face as reality hit. Liam had walked away from her forever and there wasn't a damn thing she could do to change it.

'Why didn't you go after him?' Lizzie asked, staring straight at her with her hands wrapped tight around a mug of tea in Angie's apartment.

'I don't know. I wanted to, I really did. But I couldn't get the words out of my mouth. I couldn't stand up to chase him. My whole body turned to jelly after he told me he's not over me and that he never will be.'

'You still have a chance,' Lizzie said.

'No, I don't. He told me if he walked out we were done. And what did I do? I let him walk away.' Angie stared into the mug of tea sitting on the floating island in Michael's penthouse. 'So now, not only has my marriage fallen apart, I've lost the man I love.'

'What is this really about, Angie? Because I know you don't love Michael. He breached your trust and one way or another, you're going to leave.'

Maybe Lizzie was right. She'd done everything in her power to mend her marriage, but band aids couldn't heal gaping wounds.

How could she keep trying when she didn't want to be with Michael anymore? Staying in an unhappy marriage wasn't fair to either of them.

'I know,' Angie whispered.

'So why? Why didn't you just run after Liam when you had the chance?'

Angie took a moment before answering the question. 'Because he deserves better than how I've treated him.'

Lizzie brought the mug of tea to her lips and blew on the hot water. She sipped, then placed the mug on the marble bench. 'Ange, that's so dumb and you know it. He offered his heart to you and you said no. That's on you.'

The two women stood in the kitchen, sipping their peppermint tea in silence, when Lizzie piped up. 'Did you hear that? It sounds like something's vibrating.'

Angie perked up. 'Where's it coming from?'

'The study, I think.'

They both put their mugs down and Lizzie led the way to the study. Inside the room, the buzzing got louder.

'It's coming from the wardrobe,' Angie said, storming through the large room, past the bed and into the closet. When she looked up, she noticed something vibrating on the top shelf.

'It sounds like a phone,' Lizzie said.

Angie stood on her tippy toes and ran her hand around the top shelf. She couldn't reach what was up there. She rushed back to the kitchen and grabbed a stool to stand on to get a better look.

Back at the wardrobe, she peered across the timber shelf and saw a black object in the corner. She reached out to grab it.

As Angie stepped off the stool, her stomach dropped like she was free-falling on a rollercoaster.

'It's a phone.' The Nokia phone sat lifeless in her hand. She'd never seen this phone before. There was one missed call. 'What should I do?'

'Call back,' Lizzie urged.

Angie swallowed and took a deep breath to try and loosen the knot in her stomach.

The phone rang and Angie waited for the person at the other end of the line to pick up.

'Hola. How's my sexy boyfriend?' the voice said loud and clear in what sounded like a South American accent.

'Who is this?' Angie asked.

Silence.

'Hello?' Angie pressed.

'Who is this?' the woman finally shouted back.

'I'm Michael's wife. Who the hell are you?'

The woman hung up.

Angie stared at the phone. After a minute, it all started to make sense. The long stints away from home. The sneaking around. The private phone calls in the office.

'Holy cow,' Angie whispered as she glanced at Lizzie. 'The bastard's been playing me this whole time.'

'What do you mean?' Lizzie asked.

Without answering Lizzie's question, Angie opened the text messages and began scrolling. Hundreds upon hundreds of text messages were exchanged between Michael and the woman he called Rosa.

'Jesus, Angie. Say something,' Lizzie said.

'Michael's dad is terminally ill,' Angie said, lifting her eyes from the phone. 'He has mere months to live. If these texts are anything to go by, Roger promised Michael ten million dollars on his death, but only if he stayed married to me.'

Lizzie's eyes grew large and her mouth dropped open.

'This is why he wouldn't let me leave. Why he's kept me around for so long. It's not because he loves me. He's waiting for a payday.'

The only explanation was Michael's father didn't want to see his son go through another divorce.

She knew first-hand how fast legal bills could stack up. He'd already spent a lot of money settling his last two divorces.

Then she remembered the day her card had declined when she bought a present for Jen's baby shower.

Angie stormed into the office and turned on the computer. Michael's login details were on the desktop. She keyed in the passcode to the internet banking website.

As she scrolled through the accounts, she witnessed multiple personal loans, mortgages and debts. Michael wasn't wealthy. He was almost two million dollars in debt.

Angie's hands flew to her mouth. Thank goodness common sense had prevailed when they'd gotten married. She kept a one hundred percent share to her apartment and they only had one joint account. Everything she'd worked so hard for was in her name. He wouldn't drag her down with him.

'Michael has nothing. He needs that ten million from his father so he doesn't go bankrupt.'

Lizzie stood in the doorway of the office. Her limp arms didn't move. 'Angie, you can't stay with him now.'

'No,' Angie replied as she contemplated her next move. 'I'm going to do what he never had the balls to do.'

* * *

When the click of Michael's keys unlocked the front door, Angie sat back in the leather armchair near the window of the balcony, and sipped a gin and tonic. It was dark now, past eleven p.m.

His shoes clicked against the tiles and when he reached the kitchen, he opened the fridge and pulled out a bottle of white wine.

Angie flicked on the light switch of the lamp next to the arm chair.

Michael jumped and slammed the fridge door shut. 'Christ, Angie. What the hell are you doing? I thought you'd be in bed by now.'

'Hello, Michael,' she replied as she swirled the gin and tonic in one of Michael's crystal glasses.

'Are you okay?' He asked.

'Better than ever, actually.' Angie stood up and strolled towards the kitchen slowly. 'I found out about your little mistress.'

Even with a fake tan, his red cheeks were visible in the darkness of the apartment.

'You're a cheating scumbag.'

'I—'

'Uh uh,' Angie said as she raised her hand. 'It's my time to speak. God knows you've had more than enough air time to bitch and moan about how hard this has been for you.' When she reached the kitchen, she placed the glass on the marble bench. 'I can't believe Rosa isn't even the worst of it. When were you going to tell me about your father? The money? The debt?'

Michael's faced paled. 'Angie, it's not what you think.'

Angie raised an eyebrow. 'It's not what I think?'

Having the upper hand was so powerful it sent a rush through her veins. Michael didn't stand a chance. She was a tiger in the courtroom. He couldn't argue the evidence against him.

'Let me make one thing very clear to you, Michael. I won't be part of your sick game a second longer. We're separating from today. In twelve months and one day, I'm filing for divorce. After that, I never want to see you again.'

'You cheated too,' Michael spat. 'I'm not the only one who was unfaithful.'

'You're a deceitful, conniving liar. *I* never lied to you. And at least I was honest about my intentions from the start.' She pulled the engagement ring, followed by the wedding ring, off her finger and placed them on the bench. 'I guess you'll be needing the proceeds from these given the amount of debt you're in. My lawyer will be in touch shortly. Goodbye, Michael.'

She turned on her heels and headed for the door to grab the packed suitcase. 'I'll give you three million dollars.'

Angie froze.

Three million dollars.

For a moment, she considered what she could do with that much money. But as soon as the thought came, she dismissed it. Michael was proposing a dirty deal and she wanted no part of it. Besides, she had no way to guarantee her lying husband would come good on his promise, especially with his history.

She turned and stared at Michael. The man who never loved her. The man who caused her so much heartache.

'If you think I'm going to help you get money from your dying father, you have another thing coming. He should see you for the fraud that you are. A spoiled brat who can't keep his dick in his pants. I have morals and won't be party to that kind of arrangement.' She turned back to the door and pulled up the handle of her suitcase.

'This is your last chance, Angie. What about that firm you've always wanted to start on your own? This money could help you get ahead.'

Even after all this time, Michael clearly didn't know a thing about her. While the money would certainly help, she wanted success on her own terms.

Angie turned back to him one last time. 'I feel sorry for you, Michael. You think money and material things will make you happy. It won't. Rosa will leave you once all the money's gone. And then it'll just be you, alone with your whiskey, wondering where it all went wrong.'

Angie stood even taller as she finally let go of the pain. Let go of her failed marriage. 'Let me make one thing clear. You *never* had to buy my love, but you threw it away anyway. That's on you. You may not regret it now, but you will. Eventually.'

Angie rolled the suitcase out behind her. 'You'll be hearing from my lawyer. Until then, I'll send the removalists over to get my things. Don't bother contacting me,' she said as she opened the door and stepped outside, walking away from her marriage.

Forever.

CHAPTER FIFTEEN

'I told you, he's not here.'

'When will he be back?' Angie asked for the third time.

The music boomed overhead and the banjos of the country band were strumming furiously in the background.

The guy behind the bar, Jax, claimed to be Liam's business partner and was doing a good job. He wasn't letting anything slip.

'Where's he gone?' Angie demanded as she slammed her hand on the bar.

'Listen, lady. I've heard all about you and your career. Aren't there rules about confidentiality in your line of work?. All I know is he's gone away for a while. That's all you're getting out of me.'

'He's not my client. I'm within my rights to ask.'

'And I'm within mine to refuse. So, do you want a drink or not? Because you're holding up the line.'

Angie glanced behind her and spotted the displeased faces waiting to order their drinks. If Jax wasn't going to help her, she'd have to find Liam herself.

'Fine.' As she jogged downstairs and outside to her car, she pressed her smartphone against her ear.

'Angie, what a surprise. Although it is kind of late. Something wrong?'

'Jen, I need your help. Liam's MIA. I'm trying to find him but don't know where he is. Do you know?'

'Oh, Angie.' The pity in Jen's voice was palpable. 'I don't know what to tell you.'

'Jen, please. I need to know where he is. He told me today he wanted to be with me and I said nothing. He walked out and said we were done for good. But I'm not done. I'm ready to be with him. I can't lose him!' she cried as she unlocked her car and pulled herself into the driver's seat.

Jen sighed. 'Angie, you two are meant to be together. I can't stand in the way of love. Give me twenty minutes. I'll get it out of Harry.'

* * *

'Trouble in paradise, son?'

Liam rolled his eyes and shook his head in Dad's direction. They were standing next to the truck, getting the horses ready for a brumby-spotting tour in the Snowy Mountains.

It was a big tour today. Eight horses all up. While Mum was having a chat and offering tea and biscuits to the riders, Liam and Dad were prepping the horses for the trip.

The sun was shining bright and it reminded Liam of this day one year ago. Angie's birthday. On all accounts, the day was panning out in a similar way. The weather signalled they'd have stellar weather. But Liam knew how quickly it could turn.

All he hoped was history wouldn't repeat itself. He was staying clear of the single women on the ride today.

'Watson, when have I ever been in paradise with a woman? I've got some healing to do and coming home is the best way to do it.'

Watson untied the first horse and led it over to the tailgate of the truck. 'I'm getting old and decrepit, so I can always use a hand on these tours. You do all the healing you need,' Watson said as he led the first horse up the tailgate and disappeared inside the truck.

Liam untied Magic, the tall chestnut mare, and led the horse along the gravel driveway towards the tailgate.

'You always were my favourite girl,' Liam whispered as he ran his hand down her mane. 'And you've never broken my heart.'

* * *

The tyres screeched to a halt and the car slid a few centimetres across the gravel driveway.

'Shoot!' Angie said her her body propelled forward with the force of the car.

It was much like her entrance the first time she visited Liam's family farm in Gumtree Plains. Only this time, she was on a mission to find love instead of run away from it.

She jumped out of the car and slammed the door shut before running to the front door. She knocked several times, hoping to high heaven someone was home.

'Angie?' Liam's mum said as she opened the door. 'What're you doing here?' Liam's mum didn't do a very good job of hiding the surprise on her face.

'I'm so sorry to arrive unannounced, but I need to find Liam. Do you know where he is?'

'He's gone out on a tour with Watson. They'll be back at sundown.'

'Sundown?' Angie couldn't hide the groan in her throat. This couldn't wait. She'd made him wait for so long already. A year to be exact. It was time she took matters into her own hands.

'I love Liam,' she blurted without thinking. The emotions overcame her and tears threatened to burst.

'Oh, I know you do, sweetheart. Jen told me as much.'

'This is my last chance to let him know how I feel. Can you help me get to him?'

'He'll be in and out of service. I don't know whether you'll be able to call.'

'I've already tried,' Angie replied. 'And I've left three messages. I can only think of one way to get to him.'

Liam's Mum pressed crossed her arms. 'So, what're you going to do?'

Angie looked around the farm briefly. 'Can I borrow a horse?'

* * *

'This really is a dream of mine. I've never been to the Snowy Mountains to spot brumbies. And I've never met a real-life cowboy before.' The woman with blonde hair said to Liam from under a white helmet.

'Glad to be of service,' Liam replied, half-heartedly.

What was the matter with him? There was a beautiful woman flirting with him and he had zero interest.

Guess that's what a broken heart will do.

'I'm not an all-authentic cowboy. I own a bar in Canberra.'

'Let me guess,' the woman replied. '*Cowboys*?'

Liam looked at her as she batted her thick, black lashes. She was beautiful. And even though he'd walked away from Angie yesterday, she was still all he could think about.

'How did you know?'

'A wild guess,' she replied with a wide smile.

'Liam!'

His name was called out in the distance. He looked behind him to see if he'd left one of the riders behind.

Nothing.

He shrugged and continued riding along the dirt track through the bushland in the mountains.

'Are you from Canberra too?'

Before the woman could answer, he heard his name called again.

'Did you hear that?' he asked the blonde woman.

'I think it's coming from over there.' She pointed in the direction of the voice, down the dirt track they'd just ridden.

Liam halted Magic and waited for a moment, wondering where the sound was coming from.

'Everything okay back there?' Watson called out from the front of the group.

'Yep,' Liam called back, not wanting to alarm the other riders.

After waiting another moment, he spotted something in the distance rise over the hill. It was a white helmet. Then a horse emerged.

'What's Beauty doing out here?'

'Liam, I found you!' the voice cried.

Liam's heart rate kicked up a notch and punched the air from his lungs.

Oh. My. God.

The voice was loud and clear now. Beauty trotted along the path and Angie bobbed on top, only barely holding onto the reins.

She really was an awful rider.

'Thank goodness you're here. I didn't know if I'd find you. My map reading skills suck,' she said as she pulled Beauty to a halt in front of him.

Liam stared, believing his eyes were playing tricks on him. The riders from the tour gathered around, clearly wanting to know what all the fuss was about.

Angie stared at the group of eight eyes staring back at her. She was going to have to do some serious grovelling to make up for what happened yesterday.

'What're you doing here?' he asked.

'Well,' she began, surveying the eyes staring back at her. 'I wanted to say...' she paused for a long moment.

'Yes?' Liam pressed.

Magic stomped her foot and a puff of dirt burst into the air. Even the horse was getting impatient.

Angie dismounted. When her converse shoes hit the ground, she was surrounded by dust.

She untied the helmet, pulled it off and shook her hair, allowing the blonde strands to fall past her shoulders.

The sight tightened Liam's stomach in a knot. She was still the most beautiful woman he'd ever met.

'Call me a moron, a fool, a sucker. I'm all of things because I never should've let Michael talk me into going back to that sham of a marriage.'

Was this really happening? Had Angie come after him to tell him she'd left her husband?

'Liam, I need you to know I wasn't letting you walk away yesterday.'

The words tugged at his heart. 'But you did let me walk away,' he replied as his heart thudded against his chest. 'And I told you if I walked away, it was over. Whatever *this* is between us. You can't have it both ways.'

Angie lowered her head and sighed. 'You left before I could say anything.'

'That's the problem, Angie. You didn't say anything at all. You just sat there in silence.'

The bush quietened.

Even the kookaburras stopped singing their koo-kaas.

'I can't even ride. Horses scare the living hell out of me. Do you think I would've ridden out into the bush on my own to find you if I wasn't hopelessly in love with you?'

There was a collective gasp from the riders on the tour. Liam looked behind him and noticed the women pressing their hands to their hearts.

'Liam,' the blonde woman whispered beside him.

'Yes?' He asked.

'If you love her, go get her.'

Liam took a moment to think, to process the situation. Then, he jumped out of the saddle and left Magic standing on her own with the other riders.

As he walked towards Angie, he unbuckled his helmet and dropped it on the ground. He stood a few centimetres from her face.

Was she ever going to realise converse shoes weren't appropriate footwear for riding a horse?

'Do you promise Michael is gone forever?' he asked. 'Because I won't compete with him.'

'He's not completely out of my life yet. But we're officially separated and I'm never going back to him.'

Liam took a small step closer. 'Is that the truth?'

'Yes, Liam. Would you just kiss me already?' Angie stepped forward and grabbed his hands in hers.

When their lips met, he couldn't resist a moment longer. He wrapped his hands around her waist and pulled her into his body.

When they finally came up for air, the riders cheered, and the Kookaburras began singing their koo-kaas again.

'I forgot we had an audience,' she whispered in his ear. 'That's the last thing I need today.'

'Why? Because it's your birthday?'

She nodded and looked up into his eyes. 'You know I hate birthdays.'

Liam leaned down and whispered in Angie's ear. 'You can't hate your birthday anymore.'

'Why's that?'

'Because all your birthday wishes have come true.'

Angie stared into Liam's eyes. Her eyes sparkled back at him.

She ran her hand down the stubble on Liam's face and smiled. 'I only had one wish for my birthday. I have you to thank for making it come true.'

Liam pulled the woman he loved into his arms and kissed her as the riders cheered in the middle of the Snowy Mountains.

It had taken three hundred and sixty-five days for Angie to come back to him. But waiting for her was worth every second.

About the author

Rachel Rinetti is a collector of stories, teller of adventures, lover of life and spiritual being.

From a young age, she loved telling stories and taking people on a journey. Now in her thirties, Rachel has never lost her love for storytelling and writes about love, loss, grief and triumph.

When she's not writing, you can find Rachel working in her day job as a communication professional, making soy candles, hanging at the beach, or chasing sunsets with her dog.

Follow Rachel on Facebook, Instagram, Amazon, Goodreads and join her newsletter for updates (and some freebies too).

Printed in Great Britain
by Amazon

42548979R00098